Backtrack

J. M. Guinzy Jr.

Table of Contents

Chapter 1

A leaf dyed golden-red by the autumn came tumbling upon the windowsill. Through a window white-edged and fogged over by the chill of dawn, Alan Michaels found his gaze drawn towards it. It was the little wing of a beech, he recognized, still a little green around the edges, as though it was reluctant to wholly leave the summer behind.

Alan sat in a far corner, a notebook in front of him and a pencil twirling in his fingers. A menu, with great words of cursive proudly informing the patrons of the fact of the establishment's name: Chloe's Café, stood upright on its edge. Of course, it wasn't as though Alan needed the reminder, and just as he was laying the menu to rest, up came Chloe, a steaming mug in one hand and a plate with eggs, bacon, a couple of sausages, and some toast in the other.

Chloe smiled as she set Alan's breakfast on the table. "So, how's the writing coming along?" she asked.

Alan took a sip of his coffee before replying with a shrug. "Well..." he said, allowing his eyes to fall on the blank sheet before him. He turned back to Chloe with a wry smile. "These pages have seen better days."

Chloe laughed. "Don't you worry, Alan. I'm sure you'll get into the flow of things soon enough." Just then, right when she seemed to be on the cusp of handing out some sort of motherly advice, there came the tinkle of the bell at the front door, and Chloe rushed off to greet it.

Alan wrapped both hands around the mug, savoring its warmth. With its cloud of steam tickling his nose, he took another sip of the caffeine-packed, nearly-black liquid within. It was hot enough that he couldn't quite tell what it tasted like, but that was fine by him; any warmth on such a chill morning he welcomed with glee. As Alan was reaching for his toast, his hand came up short. For a long moment it simply hung there, as though the air itself had made a grab for it and was now refusing to let go.

The reason for Alan's sudden paralysis was simple: His eyes had fallen on the webbed, canyon-like scars crazing his left hand, and his mind found itself wandering off to fetch the memory of that terrible day.

The crash that lent Alan these scars had happened a year ago, and it had been a simple one: All it had involved was an automobile, another automobile, some stupidity on someone's part (Alan couldn't quite remember whose), and two fenders sinking so deep into each vehicle's anatomy that they skinned great gashes in the leather of the back seats.

What hadn't been simple, however, was what it had done to Alan. A brain hemorrhage. Orthostatic hypotension. A terrible throbbing in his head that felt less like cluster headaches and more like cluster grenades. But none of these were what annoyed him the most. No. That honor went to the blackouts. They would come suddenly and randomly, like moles surfacing out of one of their thousands of personal tunnels, sending his vision wavering and simmering like a pool of pitch black stars. When he eventually came to, he would find himself, usually, just where he had been. But sometimes he would find himself in other places. Places he did not recognize at once. Sitting on a bench all the way across town, or walking down unfamiliar streets.

Alan felt a complaint rising up inside him, but he managed to catch it before it could quite materialize. He knew he had no right to complain; the other driver had been killed instantly. Alan had seen the pictures, and calling it gory didn't fully capture the extent of it. It had taken him a good few minutes of squinting and staring to recognize anything at all human in those photos. The fact that he, Alan, had escaped that very same crash with little more than a scarred writing hand, some headaches, and a chronic case of the sleepwalks was nothing short of a miracle.

Alan shook his head to clear it. He disliked thinking of such things; it wasn't conducive to his writing.

He hazarded a second attempt at reaching for his toast. Again his eyes fell on the scars, but he made a conscious effort to keep his glance nonchalant, as though their presence didn't bother him in the slightest.

It seemed, however, that breakfast was simply not on the menu this morning. His toast an inch away from his mouth, he froze yet again, this time from a stimulus his ears informed him of.

He turned to see Gus and Red—the only people more worthy of the title of "regular customers" than he was—locked deep in conversation. Gus was waving a newspaper a little frantically in Red's face.

"—let out a man like that. What're they thinking?" Gus was saying.

Red had one arm rested on the counter, his free hand holding a cup of coffee by the lip, swirling it with gentle elegance. "Right, right," he said, nodding sagely.

"People like these don't change. Never," said Gus. "Giving them a second lease on freedom will simply result in more tragedy."

"Mmm," agreed Red.

"If you ask me, I'll tell you that our prisons need reform. How can we—"

"So," cut in Chloe, an annoyed air to her voice. "Will you two be continuing with your verbal cryptics, or will you finally tell us lesser beings what it is you're talking about?"

Red, seeming satisfied with the intricacy with which he had stirred his drink, took a long swig. "You, Chloe," he began solemnly. "You're young. You wouldn't know about the things—the *people*—that plagued our generation." He set his cup aside and adjusted himself in his seat so he was now facing Chloe head on. "So, let me tell you.

"It was a long time ago now. Not in this town, but a couple towns over." Red stopped to take another swig. "There had been a man. A terrifically interesting man."

"That man was a murderer," Gus put in.

"Being a killer and being fascinating is not a dichotomy. They are not mutually exclusive," Red said. "The best stories have a tendency to belong to the worst people."

"Alright, but what about this man?" Chloe said, her voice tinged with curiosity. "Is he the guy they let out?"

Gus looked at her a little hotly. "You kids, you have no patience, do you?"

"Girl's just curious," said Red. "Go on, pick up where I left off."

"Right." Gus cleared his throat dramatically. "This man had been a bit of an enigma. For one thing, he had a kill count bordering on the twenties, at the very least. But in spite of that, no one's ever seen him. People dreamed of the day the cops would get their hands on him. They were sure it would make national TV, and there'd be parades and festivals for weeks and weeks to celebrate his capture." Gus smiled a wry smile. "Well, so they *thought*."

Gus stopped for a moment, gazing out the misty window with blank eyes. Alan could see Chloe watching him with some intensity, clearly eager to hear more. When eventually Gus turned back toward her, he seemed a little startled to find her staring at him.

"What?" he said.

"You were saying?" Chloe said.

Gus cocked his head to one side. "I was saying something?"

Chloe groaned and rubbed harshly at her face with both hands.

Red clicked his tongue. "Demented old fool."

"You're one to talk," Chloe said.

"Anyway," Red said, pretending not to hear, "what Gus was saying is, at some point, this man *was* caught. And—and this is the strange part—there was none of what anyone predicted. No national TV, no parades, nothing. All we got was the tiniest blurb in the local paper saying that they got him. No pictures, not even a name. People were asking the authorities; radio silence."

"But why?" Chloe asked. "Why would they hide his identity?"

"That's pretty simple, if you'd just stop and let it simmer in that young little head for a minute," said Red, making ever clearer his disapproval of the younger generation. "He was someone important. A politician, or some sort of local hero, maybe. Regardless, one thing's clear: If his identity had gotten out, it would've spelt trouble for that little town."

"Oh—" said Chloe in a bit of a childish, bouncy voice, as though she were close to singing. "How fascinating. So this guy's free now?" Red nodded. "But," Chloe said, "I don't get it. Why do you think he's so interesting? Seems like any ol' killer to me."

At that, Red shrugged. "No clue." He swirled his drink once before draining the glass. "What I *do* know is, you should be careful. With someone like that free, you can never be too safe."

Chloe stared... and stared... and stared. She stared at Red for so long that he soon became visibly discomforted.

"What, girl?" he snapped.

"This story you just told me..." she began, sparing Gus, whose eyes were still glued to the window, a glance before shifting her eyes back to Red, "You're sure it isn't something you two cooked up over in dementia land?"

Gus showed no sign at all of having heard. Red, however, startled at the boldness of the accusation, nearly knocked over his chair as he jumped to his feet.

"It isn't!" he said, exasperated. "It's all true, I tell you!" Then, quite suddenly, he pointed at Alan. Alan, unsure of what was happening, started terribly. The next thing Red said, however, made him breathe a sigh of relief. "Look! Just ask Alan! He's from those days, I'm sure he remembers."

Chloe turned to Alan, but no question seemed forthcoming. Instead, she had a wry smile separating her cheeks, as though to say, *Sorry about these two*. She let her eyes rest on Alan for a moment before turning back to Red, who was still stood up with a somewhat feral look in his eyes.

"Yes, yes," Chloe said, both hands on Red's shoulders in an attempt to guide him back into his seat. "I believe you. I'm just teasing is all."

Red eyed her with a look that clearly said he didn't believe her, but he nonetheless sat himself back down. Chloe stepped behind the counter wearing a childish grin, and just as she was about to disappear through the door that could've conceivably led to the kitchen, Gus spoke up for the first time in a while.

"You're forgetting something."

Chloe raised her eyebrows and did a double take of everything that sat atop the pair's table. "I don't think I did," she said.

"Not you." Gus nodded at Red. "Him."

"And what's that?" spat Red.

"This murderer. He had a trademark. A little something he used to throw into all his murders, like an artist signing his work." At this point, Gus fell into what seemed to be a terribly deep bout of thought, but a moment of keen observation would've revealed the truth—he was simply nodding off. Realizing the fact, Red clicked his tongue.

That little tidbit that Gus let slip seemed to arouse Chloe's curiosity. "Well?" she said, turning to Red. "What was his trademark?"

Red threw his shoulders upwards in a nonchalant shrug. Using his thumb, he daubed off a bead of coffee that had found its way up to the lip of his otherwise empty coffee cup. "I didn't forget he had a trademark. In fact, I even remember that he had a nickname, something the locals used to call him in lieu of whatever his real name was." At this point, he stopped and heaved a great sigh. "Problem is, I only remember the fact of their existence. What they *actually* were, I don't remember."

Chloe visibly deflated. "Well, if you remember, feel free to come tell me."

"Oh, don't you worry," said Red, a maniacal grin glued to his face. "As Gus said, people like these don't change. Just keep your eyes on the news, girl, and soon enough he'll show you what his trademark was himself."

Chloe gulped and offered up a nod before slinking off into the kitchen.

As soon as she was out of sight, Alan got up from his table, leaving his coffee twice-sipped and breakfast entirely untouched, and made for the spindly high chair next to Gus.

Alan's approach seemed to break Gus out of his stupor. "Eh," he said drunkenly despite not having drank. "Who're you?"

"Gus, it's Alan," said Red, shaking his head. He turned to Alan, a small, embarrassed grin on his face. "Nice of you to join us, old boy. So, what can we do you for?"

Alan was torn between buttering them up a little and getting right to the point. After a moment of deliberation, he settled on the latter. "That murderer you were talking about," Alan began. Red gave a nod, showing he was open to the topic, so Alan went on, "By any chance, would you know of any way to contact him?"

Gus nearly fell out of his chair. Red's eyes narrowed as he went pale. "*Contact* him?" he said, the suspicion apparent in his voice. "And why on earth would you want to contact a murderer?"

Alan shifted his eyes in a way that made him seem all the more suspicious. "No reason, no reason," he lied. "Just thought it would be an interesting talk."

"Alan," said Red. "Don't go searching out some mess to fall into, you hear?"

"It was just a question," Alan grumbled as he stood up. "Well, thanks anyway. Old fools," he added under his breath. And with that, he made for the diner's front door.

Right as he was about to step outside, he caught Gus muttering to himself.

"What was it...? What was it?"

The tiny sound of crumpling caused Alan to turn around. He saw Gus, lips still moving but words not forthcoming, folding up the newspaper he had been holding. He was meticulous, making sure both halves met in the perfect middle, no more, no less.

Alan felt as though something fell into place inside his head, though he wasn't sure what. Deciding he had better uses of his time than watching a demented man doing origami, Alan turned away and stepped on outside.

Alan Michaels, if you must know, was a writer. A dastardly good one, at that. Theirs was a little, insignificant town on the border of another larger but equally insignificant town, and this town, Alan's, was the type that nobody outside of it would've ever heard of.

If on the off chance someone *had* heard of it, however, Alan Michaels and his literary exploits were likely to be the reason. His early career had gone from strength to strength, putting out bestsellers one after the other.

Following his accident, however, all that had gone up in smoke. Never mind his writing hand, his brain seemed to turn from a creativity dispenser, churning out good idea one after another, into a regular old rock.

This morning, however, something snapped, because Alan Michaels...

"The best stories have a tendency to belong to the worst people."

... Knew how he would get his career back.

Chapter 2

Alan stretched as he stepped outside the diner. He looked around at all the red and yellow littering the ground, and he listened to all the pleasant crackling the dried leaves gave off as they were dragged along by the wind. For a moment his mind wandered, thinking of what a wonderful autumn morning this was, and he found himself wishing to find a bench somewhere to just while the day away.

He shook his head to snap himself out of his reverie. He had no time for this. There were things to be done: numbers to be got, talks to be had, stories to be writ. And it was as such that, on the finest autumn morning their little town had witnessed in perhaps generations, Alan Michaels' feet brought him to the local police station.

A set of wooden double doors were all that separated him from the inside. He hesitated for a short moment, then knocked three times. There was no answer, so he tried again, his knocks landing a little harder this time. Again, no answer. Feeling a little perplexed, Alan pulled the door open.

When he stepped inside, he was mildly surprised to see that the pair of cops behind the desk, both uniformed in an authoritative dark blue, were eyeing him with amused looks. The room was a fairly large one, and facing the desk were many rows of five seats, but apart from the three of them the room was empty.

As Alan made his way to the desk, he looked around in some confusion, wondering what it was that amused these two so. Only when he had seated himself on the high chair facing one of the cops did one of them speak up.

"Sir," he said, his cheek resting on his fist. "I'm not sure if you've never been to a police station before, but you don't need to knock before entering."

Alan stared blankly for a moment.

"O—Oh." Alan could feel himself turning red. He suddenly felt more than a little stupid.

"Anyway, sir," the cop said. His expression still held a hint of amusement, but the voice he put on meant business. "How can I help you today?"

"Ah, yes. I heard some concerning news this morning. About a convict—a murderer—being let out on parole."

"Yes, what about him?"

"I know this sounds absurd..." Alan trailed off to allow the man a moment to brace himself. He nodded, so Alan continued, "I'd like to talk to him. See, I'm a writer, and I was thinking that it might be interesting to have a conversation with him, just see what his thought process looks like, stuff like that. Is it possible for you guys to provide some information on him? Like an address, or a number I could contact to get in touch?"

The cop raised his eyebrows in what Alan felt was amusement. He didn't like that; he felt as though he was being belittled. Before he could mention it, the cop spoke up.

"Sir, I'm not particularly sure *why* you'd like to speak to a murderer in his own home, but, convict or not, we aren't allowed to disclose personal information." Suddenly the man sat upright, and only then did Alan realize how large he was. "Sir, I don't know what you're doing, and maybe I'm misunderstanding something here, but I'd strongly advise against seeking this man out. Even if you find him, it'll just land you in a world of trouble."

The two men sat eyeing each other for a long moment. Eventually Alan looked away, muttering something about keeping it in mind. He stood up and made for the door.

"Well," Alan said aloud as he put some distance between himself and the station, "there goes that idea." This was yet another effect of the accident—a predilection for entirely unwarranted soliloquy. He never realized he was doing it; if he had, he could've very easily stopped.

Despite what he'd told the cop, Alan did not keep his advice in mind; he had already forgotten it, in fact. There was a story to be penned down, and, by God, Alan would pen it down.

"Say, what's say we go down there, huh? Down to the old train's station," Alan said to himself.

And, truth be told, it wasn't a bad idea. His younger days had featured many an excursion to that very station, and it was for the simple reason that, in the calm and quiet that graced it, great ideas and greater thoughts flowed to him as effortlessly as a leaf flowing along a river.

But there was also another reason: His instincts told him to go have a peek, and he knew better than to distrust his instincts.

And so he did.

As he walked, the already small crowds thinned even further, soon fading altogether. Eventually he reached a part of town that was in complete disuse, and even then his feet kept stomping on. He must've walked a mile or two by now. It was a slow walk, and informing him of the passage of time was the sun, which had at some point risen to a crescendo and was now beginning to slip back toward the horizon.

From there, several more minutes of walking were enough to bring Alan to his destination. This part of town seemed straight out of a movie: There were buildings crumbling into dust, holes scarring their sides, scaffolding exposed, and thin metal beams protruding out of the sides of crumbled walls. Not a single sound but the echoing of Alan's footsteps.

And in the midst of it all was the train station, everything about it prim and proper, as though it were a mere hologram in a war-torn land, as though whatever had plagued every other part of the area had decided to steer clear of it.

Alan wandered aimlessly for a good length of time. The silence had been off-putting at first, but soon Alan found it soothing; he only wished that nothing but the crunch of his footsteps would break it.

Alan walked, and walked, and walked. He stepped inside the pitch black lobby. He slapped at the wall until his hand landed on a single switch, which he flicked on. If it was meant to inform a certain appliance within to turn on, it was failing rather miserably. Alan waited a little longer to no avail, and, seeing as it was too dark inside to even make out the opposite wall, he stepped back outside. There were no trains on the track. He stepped lightly off the ledge and onto the tracks. They held no sign of rust, as though the union of water and oxygen had simply never happened here. This lack of rust, specifically, Alan found eerie, so he climbed back onto the ledge and went on wandering, and wandering, and wandering...

It was quite by accident that he found the payphones. It felt just a touch strange to Alan, the fact that he had missed them all this time. But there they had been all along, right on the other side of the tracks, like an undiscovered village right across the local river.

Alan approached the payphones, and at once he was assaulted by a horribly pungent odor, as though a chemist had been commissioned to get in the lab and just do his worst. Alan gagged, drew his shirt over his nose, and turned to the smell: Right opposite the row of payphones were the toilets. Dilapidated or not, he couldn't imagine what would've had to have happened in there for it to reek so much.

For an odd moment, an image of the inside flashed in his mind: three stalls, four sinks with a mirror over each, three soap dispensers, and a small trash can in the corner. It was a perfectly ordinary restroom, indeed.

Except, of course, for the black-haired, open-eyed woman, dead in stall number two.

Alan started at the sight of the image behind his eyes. He shuddered and shook his head harshly.

"What the hell was that?" he said aloud.

He thought for a moment of going in and peering beneath the door, just to cure his paranoia. He stood still for a long while, deliberating, then decided against it. If—*if*—he checked, and found that the stall was indeed not empty, he had no idea what he'd do.

Alan spared the restroom a final glance before heading over to the payphones. He went over to the one right beside the ticket booth (also the one the farthest away from the restrooms), pulled open the door—in the silence, its creak sounded like the cry of a war horn in the dead of night—and stepped inside.

The silence within the booth seemed to run a layer deeper than the one outside, if that was possible. Alan picked the phone off of the receiver. He stood there for a moment, his expression blank, wondering.

And that was when he opened the envelope.

Yes, all this time, there had been an envelope. Arriving at the diner earlier that morning, Alan had found it lying on a table. *His* table. Alan had stared at it for a long moment, wondering if it was meant for *him*, before picking it up and slipping it into his satchel.

Standing in that payphone booth, he no longer wondered. That envelope *was* meant for him, evidenced by the fact that inside, there was a single slip of paper, bearing upon it a telephone number, the jagged rips on its edges giving away the fact that it had been torn from a larger sheet.

His eyes stuck to the slip in his hand, Alan raised his hand to the keypad and began firing off numbers from his fingertips. Soon, Alan was done dialing in the phone number. Whose? Alan had no clue.

The phone rang. So, the number was legitimate. Alan's heart was hammering as though it wanted nothing more in than moment than to splatter all along the inside of his ribcage.

And then something happened, happened so suddenly that Alan's stomach nearly leapt through his mouth: someone answered the phone.

"Interested?" said the deep, gruff voice.

Alan, not yet having recovered from the shock of his stab-in-the-dark call actually being picked up, blinked. "Sorry?"

"*Sorry?*" the man repeated. His voice evoked something primal within Alan, something that urged him to flee.

But, nonetheless, he stood his ground. "Excuse me, I'm not too sure who I'm speaking with."

There was a chuckle. "You know exactly who this is. You were searching me out, weren't ya?"

Alan felt himself black out. "Y—You're the... killer?" he said, feeling unsure about the word "killer", in case the man took offense.

"Bingo." Alan could hear the cold grin in the man's voice. "And you, let me guess. You're someone who's, one way or another, attempting to exploit my past for your own financial gain, yes?"

Alan was taken aback. Not by *what* he said, which was true enough, but by *how* he said it; Alan's image of a murderer involved a big guy, pure black sunglasses, spiked up hair, face in a snarl, and also some spikes on the shoulders for added effect. He thought murderers had maniacal, simian laughs and a distinct difficulty in stringing together a grammatically correct sentence involving more than four words. So when this man—this cold-blooded murderer—churned out a sentence that was, for honest lack of a better word, eloquent, it startled him to a terrible degree.

The murderer, probably mistaking Alan's startled silence for an admission of guilt, said, "Yeah, I figured as much. Not the first time either. Hell, the damn warden that oversaw my release told me to get someone to document my kills. Said, messed up as I am, my mind works in a fascinating way. Well, I agree on both parts, but maybe not the way he'd expect." And there was the maniacal laugh. It sent a shiver down Alan's spine, but it also eased his nerves a little. His idea of what a murderer was like was at least somewhat on the mark.

Alan cleared his throat and said, "Well, see, that's exactly what I'm calling about. I think your mind is fascinating, too—"

"Wouldn't *you* think that, buddy."

"—and I'd like to know more about your thought process with regards to your murders. For example, how do you decide who your victims'll be, why and how you'll kill them, and also what you gain from all this?"

"What I gain, eh?" There was a long silence on the line, and soon Alan began to harbor an irrational fear that the man would find a way to sneak inside the booth he was in and twist his neck off. Eventually, however, the man spoke up. "There's an incredible rush that comes with killing someone: being the very first person to know of their death. It's an indescribable feeling, as if, for that one moment, I'm some sort of god. As if all the power in the universe belongs to me.

"In my younger days, I used to invite people out of bars or clubs to dinner. I'd pay for takeout—believe me, you'd be surprised how stupid some people can become if they get a free meal. We'd take the food and go into someplace secluded, but not suspicious. I used to like this one particular bench at the park. It had a lamp right overhead, giving them a false sense of security, but what they didn't realize was how poorly that light carried; as long as you were quiet, you could easily stab someone to death in that light, and all someone, say, a hundred feet off would see was a bit of movement.

"Anyway, I'd kill them, then I'd sit there imagining their families, thinking about how they were completely oblivious to the fact that this person, who had been alive and happy not three hours ago, was now dead. I'd invent conversations, like, Mom says, 'Wow, she's really late today, isn't she?' and Big Sis goes, 'Don't worry Mom, she sometimes falls asleep at her friend's homes. I'm sure she'll be home in the morning.' Little do they know, by the time morning rolls around, Lil' Missy's head and torso will be in two separate zip codes."

There was a long silence. Usually, Alan would be eager to fill it, but at the moment he was just too stunned. He knew he was talking to a murderer, so it wasn't as though he didn't expect some degree of insanity. But this? This, he didn't expect in the slightest.

"That's..." Alan began, discovering his voice after what felt like minutes. "That's sick."

"How nice of you to notice."

"I—I—" stammered Alan, his stomach still lurching from what he'd just heard. Right about now, he was truly starting to wonder if he had the stomach to see this book through. "I think I'll just leave for now. Thank you for your time." Alan was about to put down the receiver, but something kept him from pulling the phone away from his ear. There was a silence that seemed to last a minute.

"You're still here, I see." The voice didn't seem to be poking fun; it was just a statement. "Well, while you're here, I may as well tell you the brief portfolio of one of my kills. Young woman—couldn't have been older than thirty. Florist. She severely disliked her blond hair, so she dyed it, but to what color escapes me. She disliked standing out, so I'd guess black. I poisoned her with something akin to acid; her stomach must've been shredded, and if she'd thrown up, her lips and gums would probably be missing. I wouldn't know though, since, to the best of my knowledge, the body was never found."

And then, despite his promise of keeping things brief, the murderer proceeded to tell Alan about the events that had led to the two's meeting, the events that transpired following the meeting, and also some small, uninteresting details about the murder itself.

Only one thing at all stood out to Alan: For the fact that she had been a florist, the murderer had drawn a pair of flowers on her cheeks. When that information was divulged, Alan all of a sudden found his eyes being dragged in a particular direction: the restrooms.

"That's all I have time for right now," said the murderer at last, after what must've been over an hour. "Tuesday. Same time. Same place."

It took Alan a moment to figure out what was happening: He was being told when their next talk would be. Alan jotted down the details of it on his hand, then placed the receiver down. He didn't particularly care about the next meeting.

Alan turned around, pushed open the door to the booth, and began making his way home. In front of the restrooms he stumbled hard, and as soon as he had righted himself, he picked up his pace.

The image of the bathroom, along with its lone inhabitant, came back to him, this time a tad more detailed. She was black-haired, open-eyed, missing both lips, and had a pair of red, red roses drawn onto her cheeks.

Once Alan was far enough away that the silence no longer felt oppressive, he cast a furtive look back over his shoulder, half expecting the bathroom door to be hanging on its hinges and the corpse of a woman to be dragging itself along after him.

But there was nothing but a calm, quiet train station. And so, not wanting to tempt fate, Alan picked up his pace to a slow jog and made his way on home.

Chapter 3

The walk back seemed to enervate Alan about twice as heavily as the walk to. That could've been put down to a few factors, the most likely suspect being the fact that Alan now had to carry the weight of more than just himself; he knew of a murder that no one else did. The murderer may have already served his time, but, still, Alan felt that the victim deserved a proper send off. One that, unfortunately, she would never get.

The sun had by now sunk down halfway beneath the horizon. People soon began to reappear, but those of the specific occupation Alan was seeking out didn't appear for another couple blocks.

Eventually, right by a little delicatessen he had somehow never noticed before, Alan found one; the man sat in his faded yellow car with the windows rolled down, smoking. Atop the vehicle was a little wedge that read TAXI.

"Hey!" Alan said as soon as he was within earshot. The man glanced over without moving his head, a lighter held to the cigarette dangling from his lips. "Are you waiting on anyone?" Alan asked.

"Nah," the man said. "Ya got somewhere to be?"

Alan wrenched open the door and sat himself in the seat right behind the driver's. "Yeah. I'd appreciate it if you could take me home."

The man nodded, then for a long, long while did nothing more. Alan watched as he blew an occasional pall of white smoke out of the open window. For a couple minutes this was all that happened, and soon Alan began to feel a little awkward, wondering what on earth was going on.

At last, perhaps sensing the tension that had formed in his car, the driver craned his head around his seat to look at Alan. "Well?"

"Well, what?"

"Whaddya mean, 'Well what?'" he said, sounding a little annoyed. "I can't be takin' ya anywhere if I don't know where I *should* be takin' ya, can I?"

"Like I said, home," Alan repeated with all the conviction in the world.

The driver narrowed his eyes. "I ain't the Yellow Pages. Give me an address."

"Oh," Alan said, at last realizing his mistake. "It's..." he trailed off, "It's..." he began again, but the results were unchanged. For a long while Alan simply sat in stunned silence, wondering how he could've possibly forgotten his own address; following his accident, memory loss had been one of the few mental conditions that had the decency to leave him unplagued, but it seemed as though that was no longer the case.

"'Ello?" said the cabby, causing Alan to jump a little. "Everything okay back there?"

"I'm fine, I'm fine," said Alan, though the slight quiver in his voice took away any credibility the statement might've held. "My stomach's just acting up all of a sudden. You know, on second thought, I think I'll just walk. Sorry about this." He offered up a weak smile, but it came out sickly.

He stepped outside, shut the car door, and sped off as quickly as his feet would take him.

"What a day," Alan said aloud.

He had no clue how to get back home from his current whereabouts, so he decided to take a rather simple minded approach: he'd first go to Chloe's Café, and from there he reckoned his feet should have no trouble carrying him home.

And for the first time in what felt like ages, Alan was actually right about something.

Once, he ventured head-on into a dead end, and a couple of times he stumbled when his eyes fell on an unfamiliar store front. Apart from these, though, his walk home was smooth and went without hiccups. The surroundings—the ambience—seemed glaringly different to what he was used to, enforcing Alan's idea about his freshly onset dementia. Nonetheless, his feet were sure of their way. Having stomped to and fro between his home and the diner for decades now, his muscles provided directions far better than his brain.

His face lit up the second he spotted his home in the distance. He picked up his pace just a little, and soon his feet found themselves standing upon the large wiry mat that read "Welcome" in large, friendly letters.

He tried the knob, but it simply jiggled without giving way. He checked under the mat, the typical hiding spot for a spare key, but there was nothing but concrete. Alan snooped around in pots and around garden walls for a little longer, to no avail, so at last he knocked.

From within came the distinct noise of shuffling. A moment later the door came open just the smallest amount, held from going any further by a chain. The dark of dusk kept Alan from making out anything in that dark wedge. The eye peered at Alan for a short moment—then there was a terrific gasp.

The door shut, the chain unclicked, and a woman threw her arms over his shoulders in a great, big hug.

"Hello, Nala," said Alan.

The woman said nothing in reply. She just stood there sniveling and quivering, startling Alan quite a bit. He felt this was a bit of an overreaction; he hadn't even been gone that long, had he?

Soon enough the woman calmed sufficiently to at least invite him inside.

"Just sit down, Alan, just sit down," said Nala, before rushing off into the kitchen. Alan heard the clanging of pots and pans and the click of the stove being brought to life, and a moment later began the sounds of slicing and sizzling, among other things.

Fifteen minutes later his wife emerged from the kitchen with a steaming plate in hand. She set it down before him with exaggerated care, as though she were a fledgling chef hoping to impress her superior.

"Thank you," Alan said, grateful but a little confused. As he ate, Nala just stood there, watching. It made him a little uncomfortable, but he was too famished to really care; it was, after all, his first meal of the day.

"How about a bath?" Nala said as soon as Alan had shoveled the last of his dinner into his mouth.

"Sounds good," Alan said. He straightened himself up and began to head upstairs, but Nala cut ahead of him and went into the bathroom first. There was a short bout of silence, then the sound of running water; she was running him a bath.

Alan shook his head as though he were trying to beat his brain to sludge. He didn't understand this at all. He didn't have much time to think about it either, for it was hardly a moment later that Nala reemerged and beckoned him in.

Today, Alan was certain, was the most nonsensical day he'd ever had the displeasure of being a part of. An odd story from the local eccentrics for breakfast, knocking on the door of the police station, a conversation with a full-fledged killer when most would be throwing back their lunch (with the added bonus of learning of a murder that no one else knew about), having his own address slip his mind, and finally, this.

As he sank into the hot bath, he couldn't help but feel that this was the strangest part of today. He couldn't imagine why his wife was being so nice to him. She tended to be a you-do-you sort of person; if she wanted stuff done, she'd do it herself, and the same for Alan. For her to do all this, unprompted, was not just odd, it was unprecedented.

Alan stepped out of the bath, toweled himself off, and stepped into a fresh set of clothes. When he stepped outside, he found Nala sitting on the edge of the bed, a look of mild concern on her face.

"How do you feel, Alan? Is everything alright? Does it hurt anywhere?"

"Huh?" Alan said, looking himself all over for anything resembling a cut or bruise. "Why would it hurt?"

"I'm just asking." She patted the bed. "For now, just lay down and relax. I'm sure your muscles could use some loosening up after all this time."

All this time? Alan thought, taken aback. I *wasn't gone a week. Hardly that long at all, and that's "all this time" to her?*

Nala patted the bed again. "Alan, come along now. You deserve to rest well tonight."

A bulb lit up in Alan's head. He knew what this was. She was mad at him, and instead of simply telling him, this was her sarcastic, roundabout way of showing it, her way of making him figure it out.

"What'd I do?" Alan asked; he didn't feel quite up to these games just now.

Nala cocked her head. "What?"

"I did something, right? What was it?"

Nala eyed Alan with genuine confusion for a moment. Then, in an instant, that very same look was replaced with one of pity. She got up from the bed and threw her arms around him.

"Your accident," she said softly, her head rested in the crease of his neck. "It really took a lot out of you, didn't it?"

Now it was his turn to eye her (well, the back of her head, at least) in confusion. "What're you talking about?" he said. He was close to saying more, but he managed to catch himself—*Why bring up the accident?* The feeling that she was trying to insult him suddenly subsided; if that had been her intention, she wouldn't have brought up something so serious. But that just confused him all the more. If there *was* a line that connected his accident to whatever was happening at present, then Alan was failing rather miserably at finding it.

He was snapped out of his stupor by Nala's voice. He suddenly became aware that she had been speaking to him all this while.

"Alan," she said, her eyes filled with what could've only been worry. "Seriously, come lie down. You need to rest." Alan noted the hint of desperation in her voice, as though she were close to pleading.

Alan sighed. He had meant to begin penning down the start of his new book now that he had managed to acquire some details right from the horse's mouth, but this threw a rather spectacular wrench in that plan. Seeing Nala like this made his heart ache, so at last he gave in to her wishes and sprawled himself face-down in bed.

Hardly two minutes in, however, any reluctance he held vanished, and all thoughts about the book yet unwritten—the very book that would right his spiraling career—had drifted off to some place out of his mind's reach. It'd been so long since he'd gotten a massage of any sort that he had forgotten all about the joys of them.

Nala's massages always hit the spot; though her physique didn't let it on, her upper body strength was remarkable. Alan had no clue when or how she had acquired it, but he appreciated it; she was the type of woman you could count on to change a tire, for instance.

While she was squeezing between his shoulder blades, undoing a knot that had been there for God knew how long, Alan began to nod off. The warm bath had drawn out his lethargy—closer to languor than lethargy, in fact—and this just amplified it a hundred times over.

"Alan," Nala said, her voice as soft as though she were speaking to a child.

"Mm?" he said, less than half awake.

"Have a good sleep, Alan. You deserve it." She planted the gentlest of kisses on his temple, then ruffled his hair. "Sweet dreams."

And it was as such, entirely clueless as to why his wife was being so nice to him, and with vague dreams of his turbulent career being nudged back on track, that Alan Michaels drifted off into a deep sleep that night. And, though he didn't realize it, it was the first time in many, many years that his sleep was one of peace.

Chapter 4

The next Tuesday, Alan woke before the sun was up—woke, what's more, without a single nervous tingle in his tummy.

Nala's enthusiasm toward anything related to him was still intact, as was his cluelessness as to the reason for the sudden appearance of this facet of her otherwise unchanged personality. On several occasions he had considered asking her, but the question never quite managed to leave his lips, for the simple reason that he wouldn't let it. He had an odd feeling, not based on anything in particular, that he wouldn't like the answer.

So, it was as such that, peering out the dark, frosty window in the kitchen that faced far off into the reddening east, Alan sat sipping his coffee (homemade; he had decided last night not to head to the diner for today). He was pleased with this arrangement, unaware that, at that very moment, he was forgetting instead to attend to something just a little bit more pressing.

Nala came downstairs not too long later, though she looked none the happier about it; she still seemed awfully groggy, a hot shower and some cold water on her face having done nothing to rouse her.

There *was* something, however, that abated all her lethargy in an instant: the sight of Alan at the table quietly sipping away at his drink. She walked up behind him, circled her arms around his neck, and gave him a peck on the cheek.

"Morning, Alan," she said as she grabbed a cup of coffee and sat down next to him.

"Yup, morning, Nala." While he was unsure as to what had brought on her sudden change, he had decided that he would just take it in stride. By now he'd grown accustomed to it, and was even beginning to enjoy it. A bubbly Nala wasn't bad, really.

Without saying a word, Alan started to get up. He thought he could do with some toast this morning, and he decided to go and make it himself. Nala, however, did not humor him. As soon as the scraping of his chair reached her ears, as though she had read his mind, she got up herself, sliced off a couple of slices from the great loaf that sat in the corner, and dropped them into the toaster.

Nala returned carrying a plate with three slices of toast, burnt to the exact shade of black that Alan liked.

Several silent minutes later, as Alan was to-and-froing between his toast and his coffee, Nala said something that sent Alan wondering.

"Y'know, most people really hate Mondays, 'cause of stuff like work and school. But, me, I'm not a fan of Tuesdays. For starters, the supermarkets are always overcrowded, since most major restocking happens on Monday night."

Alan missed approximately half of her sentence; specifically, the part that followed the word "Tuesday".

Alan sat crunching away at his toast, sending crumbs cascading back onto his plate, his eyebrows lowered just the smallest amount.

Tuesday, he thought. It brought nothing in particular to mind, so he tried again. *Tuesday. Tuesday. Tuesday.* He could've sworn someone else had said the word to him recently, but for the life of him he couldn't have told you why he thought someone would've uttered the word Tuesday to him unprompted.

The word Tuesday was beginning to sound less and less like a real word to him, so, to take his mind off of it, he decided to turn on the radio that sat on the corner of the counter.

This station, whichever one it was, seemed to be the one to have put the "ad" in "radio". In ten minutes of listening, they had heard a grand total of zero songs. Alan's irritation grew, and at the very same instant that he was beginning to change to a different station, an ad for some sort of burger joint came on. It disappeared in a sudden crackle, and moments later the pleasant noises of jazz streamed out of the speakers.

Spurred on by the fleeting ad, Nala said, "You know, there's no good fast food places in town. You'd think after all these years they'd have had at least a couple, but no." She took a sip out of the other side of Alan's mug. "God, I'd kill for a good burger right now."

Alan's eyebrows sank even farther down his forehead, nearly meeting the top of his lashes.

Kill, huh. Kill. Tuesday. Tuesday. Kill on a Tuesday...

And then, quite suddenly, Alan remembered! Today was the day of the talk he had scheduled with the murderer!

He stood and knocked his chair over in his panic. Noticing the strange look Nala gave him, he picked his chair off of the ground and replaced it, as casually as he could make it seem. He feigned a yawn and a long stretch over his head, then glanced at the clock: a quarter past seven. His meeting was to take place at ten.

"Well," he said in an attempt to act casual, although it came out a little squeaky. "I'm gonna head on out, Nala. Need to find some inspiration for my writing."

Nala narrowed her eyes the tiniest bit, as though she knew something was off but wasn't quite sure what.

"Alright, Alan. Please, stay safe. Try and stay out of trouble if you can." She blew him a kiss from across the table. Alan smiled back at her. He headed out of the kitchen and into the living room, got his overcoat from off its hook, and then headed out the front door.

His legs ached at the thought of breaking into a run, but he fought it off. The running would only begin once his home was out of view; exactly as the murderer had put it, all Alan was doing here was not only exploiting *one* person's past, but exploiting the deaths of (if Red's estimate had been correct) at least several dozen. All for the sake of a blasted career, just so he could rake in a few more dollars. It wasn't simply distasteful, it was downright depraved; if anyone but himself had been found doing just this, Alan would've been calling for a jail term.

Alan looked over his shoulder. The house was no longer in view, so he turned back around, threw on his hood, and began to brisk walk. A couple of miles to cover, and hardly two and a half hours to cover them. It was possible, of course—in fact, Alan would be inclined to say it was easy. He just resented the fact that he could've avoided this entire rush if he had just remembered to write it down.

Alan's progress remained steady up until he arrived at the delicatessen where he had seen the cabbie. At that point, he spotted something—some*one*—that made him freeze. He was struck by a sudden pang of fear, which was terribly odd, considering Alan had gone actively seeking out such a person.

It was a cop.

He had a cell phone to his ear, and he was speaking into it as loudly as if he were giving a speech without a microphone.

Alan didn't understand it himself, but something within him rejected this man. The cop was peering into the display of a store on the same side of the street as Alan himself was walking, and all the man had to do was turn to his left and he'd be eye to eye with him.

Something told him to scoot before that happened. Simply continuing his journey down this street was a momentary consideration, but he decided against it: the display would reflect his presence, and even if the cop took no notice, the mere possibility that he could be spotted made the thought unattractive to him. Walking smoothly, no sudden movements, Alan crossed over to the other side of the street.

A date with a murderer awaited, and Alan was starting to get dangerously short on time. In the end, he decided to just slink into an alleyway. He took a few twists and turns, as though attempting to shake off any pursuers (of which there were a grand total of none) then reemerged on a street that was entirely foreign to him.

It took him no less than ten minutes of mental mapping and circumnavigating to return to his intended trail. By then, the sun said that it couldn't have been any earlier than nine, and Alan, having another mile to cover, broke into a jog.

The eerie yet soothing silence of the station greeted him. Panting hard, Alan crossed the tracks and rushed to the farthest payphone, not so much as flinching at the rancid odor of the restrooms.

He punched in the number then leaned himself against the wall of the booth. Just like last time, the phone rang. Alan waited, and waited...

And then there came the voice. He had been expecting it, of course, but the suddenness of its arrival nonetheless startled him.

"You're late," growled the voice.

"Yes, I know. My apologies"

The man chuckled in a way that sounded almost condescending, but not quite. "What, little boy forgot to write it down on his time table?"

Alan did not reply. He was too busy thinking about something else. See, even during their previous meeting, one particular characteristic on the murderer's part had stood out: his voice. Last time, Alan had been too bewildered by the fact that he was speaking to an actual convicted murderer, too disconcerted by all the terrible things he had told him, to notice.

But now the man's voice stood stark in the foreground of Alan's mind. He couldn't help the feeling of familiarity he held toward it, as though the two had been having secret, now-forgotten conversations for years prior to that first phone call. The idea that someone Alan knew could've been a cold-blooded killer was too much for him to handle, so he stowed the thought away into a faraway corner of his mind and hoped that it would hurry up and collect dust so he could lose it for all eternity.

"Hello?" said the murderer, startling Alan back to himself. "You still there?"

"Yes, I'm here. Sorry about that. Was just organizing my thoughts."

"See, that's what distinguishes someone like me from people like you. My thoughts? A mess. Complete disarray. But that's the fun of it. It's the root of my insanity. If ever I went and filed my thoughts into wherever they belonged, I would lose my insanity. I'd just be a normal, boring ol' piece of society's big jigsaw puzzle."

Alan was again struck by how articulate the man was, but this time he did not allow it to fluster him.

"Sir, if you don't mind, I'd like to discuss your thought process behind the murders you commit. I'm not particularly interested in your societal views."

"Ooh," said the killer, as though he was genuinely impressed by something. "Little boy is only offering up his voice, so he thinks I can't get at him, eh?" Alan felt a terrible shiver at those words, but before they had even subsided, the murderer had moved on. "My murders, eh?" There was a long, long pause, before he spoke again—and, when he did, it was odd. "I'm thinking of a number between one and three, both inclusive. Pick one."

Alan narrowed his eyes, shrugged, then said, "Okay, then. I pick—"

"Ah!" said the murderer.

"Y-yes?" stuttered Alan, startled.

"You're a writer, correct? So you must know about that echo chamber advice that amateurs love to toss around and other amateurs take way too seriously, right?" The man snorted derisively before going on, "'Show, don't tell', they say. Now, that's exactly what I want you to do."

"Sorry, I don't think I follow," said Alan, honestly lost.

"See, it's simple. Number between one and three. Don't *tell* me. Hold up your fingers and *show* me."

Alan's heart gave a terrible *twang*. He slowly turned around, half-expecting to see the man staring at him from right outside his booth. But there was nobody. In fact, as Alan threw his eyes all around the station, high and low, there seemed to be nothing alive in the vicinity apart from himself.

"I'm waiting." The murderer's voice sounded a mix of amused and impatient.

His heart racing, Alan held his balled fist up in the air. He was just about to hold up his fingers when he got an idea: He moved his fist behind his back and held up a peace sign.

Without a moment of hesitation, the voice said, "Two, huh?" Alan felt his breath catch from fear, but he had no time for it, because the voice went on, "Good choice. The worst choice would've been three."

"Why?" said Alan. "What's so bad about whatever was three?"

"Oh, don't you worry. We'll get there eventually, on a different day, and when that happens, you'll know." Alan shivered, and the voice coughed once into the receiver. "Anyway. Two.

"Very short man. He thought he stood out—he did, but not through any effort of his own. He had hair dyed pink, see. Kind of stuck up. Being stuck up and having no way to back it is never a good idea. Motivation behind this kill is obvious: I wanted to show the guy who's boss. So I cornered the guy in his own bathroom—at least, that's what I'd wanted people to think. I'd planted some of his blood in his bathroom, but in truth, everything had happened by a dumpster in some random alley. Anyone pass by, they'd only see me, not a pixel of him—the dumpster wasn't all the way in the corner, so I squeezed him into that little gap so that the dumpster would hide him from view. Placed my hand around his throat... I expected something resembling a fight, at least. I'm not sure if the squeeze hampered his mobility, or he was just naturally in possession of the worst upper body strength I've ever seen... You're following along still, yes?"

"Yes, I am. Don't worry, I'll stop you if I get lost."

Alan, in fact, was more than following along. He felt as though he were watching a movie, so clear were the images before his eyes. The perks of being a writer, he supposed. Spending hours upon hours lost in your own mind tended to provide a more vivid imagination.

"Good," said the murderer. "Can't have you getting lost now. Anyway, there's the guy, barely putting up a fight while my hands are crushing his windpipe. Left the world without even popping a squeak, bless him."

Alan nodded. He could see the body before his eyes, lips and extremities faded blue, eyes wide with a mix of non-understanding and fear, stuffed into that corner like packing paper stuffed into a box.

"What did you do with the body?" asked Alan. "You didn't just leave it there, I hope?"

"Before anything else, I carved a big X on each of the guy's palms. Took me a while, that. Had to make sure they were identical. As for where I put the body... Well, let's put it this way: the cops could only undeniably catch me after my kill count had gone well into the twenties—quarter of a century, that. Suffice it to say, I know where to stow my corpses."

Alan nodded, then asked, "The Xs you carved, was there a reason for that?"

"My trademark. Just letting the fools know I was there."

Alan found himself a little confused by this. "But, the one you told me about the other day, you didn't carve an X. It was flowers then, yes? I'm not quite getting what your trademark is here."

The man cackled in a way that seemed rather badly disjointed for someone as well-spoken as himself. "Think about it," he said. "Believe me, the answer's not as deep as you might be diving for right about now."

"Oh." Alan felt that this was a little too terse, but he decided to roll with it. "Well, thank you for your time today. Would you be interested in meeting again sometime soon?"

The murderer smacked his lips a few times, then said, "I'll be busy for a while. What's say, a month from now? The day the Lord Himself was born, Christmas. Xmas, if you will. Now, how's that for a present under the tree?"

"I can make that work, I'm sure. Same time?"

"Same time."

"Alright then, thanks again for your time, sir. I'll be on my way now. Talk to you in a month."

With that, Alan placed the receiver down. And only at that point did he notice that his hand was still behind his back, but it was no longer a peace sign on display. Instead, his middle finger was now lying flat across the middle of his index finger, and the shape of it could only be described as an X.

Chapter 5

It had been an autumn unlike any other, but it was now, unfortunately, coming to an end. Though the ground lay red and orange like the wood of a bonfire, the trees themselves had all but done their shedding, and they now lay bare and bald, their boughs prepared for the winter snow to adorn them.

Alan Michaels, as was customary, had whiled away both the morning and the afternoon at Chloe's, and was now dealing the same fate into the evening. The smell of his steaming toast wafted in the air, but he left it alone for now, instead opting for a long draught of coffee.

He looked out the fogged-over window at the naked trees. Seeing them so bare sent a winter-fueled shiver up his spine, so he pulled his hood up and huffed into his bare hands—he had spent a good chunk of the morning trying to find a pair of mittens, but evidently came short.

Alan turned his attention to the book that lay before him. He hadn't, in fact, *meant* to waste his day like this. He had come here this morning with all the conviction in the world, ready to finally put pen to paper on his new book—and pen to paper it indeed was, for Alan was as old school as old school went. He *did* own a typewriter, but the old, beat-up specimen was at present sitting in his closet and collecting dust. No, to him, the first draft had always been heart to pencil to paper, the typewriter only coming out of hiding once everything was penned down.

However, his inactivity was not the result of any sort of laziness. He had no clue why, but he found himself awfully tired today. More tired than he had felt walking all those miles on two separate occasions. To a degree, he regretted not sleeping in; his legs ached, his arms crackled, his palms were torn. Hell, even his fingers had odd pins and needles to them, resulting in his pencil twirling only happening at odd, jittery intervals, for if he did it any quicker, he would drop his pencil. And to top it off, his back hurt too. If he happened to drop something, it would have to stay there for a while.

Still, he had some good ideas, so he was reluctant to call the day a *total* waste. Seeing, however, as over two hours later the graphite of his pencil had never met the sheet before him on a single occasion, this day could, if he were honest, only be filed away in the "Waste" section.

Alan placed his pencil down with a click, then sighed. How long would he prolong this whole ordeal, he wondered. Two talks. Two entire talks with a murderer in the flesh, and still he could not come up with a combination of words that he thought would amount to a fitting first line. It didn't just annoy him, it angered him, and it was a sort of anger only other writers would understand. After all, he could wring the details of all the murders out of all the serial killers in the country if he wanted to, but it was equivalent to nothing if he never put it on paper.

He picked his pencil back up and began fiddling with it. Without looking, he began doodling on the page. Just then, from across the room he caught Chloe's voice. She seemed to be placating a very riled up Gus—Alan would've bet everything he'd written today that she had just accused him of making up one of his stories.

Alan was trying to make out the details of that conversation—a futile effort from this far away— when there came a tinkle as the front door swung open. In wandered a young man, both his arms occupied with a tottering stack of newspapers.

"Papers!" called the man. Several people, one of them Red, scurried forward. Alan considered the man with a mixture of intrigue and confusion. He had never heard of papers being delivered at such a time. Well, whatever. He tended to dislike the news anyway, choosing to steer clear of it whenever possible. Today, however, something told him to give the poor thing a shot, see what it had to say. There *was* something in there worth seeing today, his instincts told him, so he got up, took a paper from the top of the stack, dropped a dollar into the little bag hooked on the man's belt, and returned to his seat.

It'd been quite some time since Alan had last let his eyes feast upon the inside of a newspaper. His heart twanging with nervous excitement,

Alan flipped to the first page. He performed a quick, perfunctory scan of the page, found nothing of note, then turned to the next page and repeated the process. And again. And again. And again.

Politics. Politics. Sports. Politics. Some community work. Cartoons. Ads. Politics. Politics. Alan would've been hard pressed to name a single politician in their entire town, so how there was always politics on the news was lost on him.

Such a mind-numbing task all this sifting was that by the time Alan arrived at the last page, he was beginning to nod off. His scanning had by now gone from perfunctory to just flat out lazy. Now it was nothing more than a quick, lazy glance at each headline, then off to the next page.

Flip. Three pages to go. *Flip.* Two pages. *Flip.* One... *Flip...* And that was it. His feeling had been incorrect; there had been nothing interesting at all about this. Heaving a heavy sigh, Alan flipped the paper shut—and there, on the back page, was an article.

It was a strange piece of writing, to put it mildly. Not so much the content, which he hadn't yet read, but more—well, everything else.

To begin with, it wasn't printed on any conventional medium, but something sort of soft, more akin to a sheet of paper towel than any paper Alan knew of.

Then there were the words. Not the font gracing the rest of the paper, but one that seemed close to cursive.

Alan was a shrewd individual, more so than his demeanor would let on. His shrewdness did not leave him this morning, for he noticed these things in an instant. What had instead left him was plain old common sense, for the simple fact that, despite his noticing these oddities, he did not for a second think anything of them.

Filing it away as the press having run out of paper (he didn't quite realize how unlikely this assumption was), Alan began to read:

11/26

MAN MURDERED IN HIS HOME.

Block 1100, Franklin, a local man was found dead in the first floor bathroom of his home. While autopsy reports have not yet surfaced due to an undisclosed delay, leading investigators believe the murder to have taken place in the early morning, likely between the hours of three and four. However, neighbors claim that there had been no disturbances or out-of-place noises between said hours. While many likely causes of death have been discussed, experts agree that the most plausible one is asphyxiation.

Alan, tired as he was, noticed nothing particularly alarming about this. Just another report on any ol' tragedy. Nothing out of the ordinary.

A single line down, however, Alan found that opinion flipped on its head.

The man, identified as having bright-pink hair, was a banker by profession. His neighbors describe him as being a very outspoken man, but not an ill-natured one.

The cadaver's hands each had the letter "X" carved into them. Some experts indicated that they believed the murder to be religiously motivated, with the X representing a cross, perhaps in mocking allusion to Christianity. This conjecture was quickly put to rest by friends and relatives, who claim that the man was a fervent atheist. While experts have provided conjectures as to the motivation behind the murder, the truth of the matter remains unknown.

It was a remarkably short article given the weight of the topic. And yet, by the time Alan's eyes had landed on that final word, goose bumps had raised, eyes had widened, and a terrible, sinking feeling had settled in his stomach. The last coherent thought Alan managed to have, right before he was engulfed in a panicked frenzy, was this:

This seems awfully familiar, doesn't it?

In a bit of a clueless stupor, his heart hammering like a caffeinated woodpecker, Alan stood up, lifting his chair as he did so. He usually allowed it to scrape the ground, but today he felt no need to draw attention to himself, at which that screech would have done a wonderful job.

Alan stepped outside the diner, vaguely aware of the bell tinkling overhead, marking his exit. The air was filled with the chill of winter in the making, but it did not hold a candle to the icy lump in his stomach.

The murder had taken place earlier today—the morning of the twenty-sixth of November.

His talk with the murderer had been on the twenty-second.

"Alright," he said, not only failing to hear himself, but also failing to realize he had even said anything. "What shall we do about this?"

Of course, it was mostly rhetorical; Alan knew the answer before he had even thought up the question. He had a sinking feeling that he knew what was happening here. But he didn't want to jump to any conclusions, especially if someone else's freedom was on the line. It could, after all, have been a coincidence. A coincidence to the most astronomical degree, to be sure, but a coincidence nonetheless.

Before anything else, he would have to find out what was going on here. And there was only one thing for it: The two had made an appointment for Christmas, sure, but it seemed as though Alan would have to bring that forward.

By the time his brain had thought this, his feet, ever the primal thing, had already carried him over a quarter of the way to the old station.

Alan hated walking, and cardio, and really anything that had the prospect of lengthening his lifespan. And yet, there he was, puffing along a couple mile stretch as quickly and efficiently as though his lungs were metal, his heart fine rubber.

And just like that, he had arrived. He had arrived... He had... Yes, he had arrived, indeed...

But where?

Alan looked around. It was the train station. Of course it was—why, just look at the wholly, inexplicably rust-free tracks.

Alan stepped off of the platform onto these, traversed them, and then heaved his way up onto the other side. And there he stood for a long, long while, gazing into a certain dark room, unmoving, barely breathing.

It was the old train station. He was sure of it now. There was a scarce chance, after all, that anywhere else could he find such a revolting smell as the one streaming out of these restrooms.

He turned aside and began his slow, slow walk to the farthest payphone, all the while wondering to himself. If it *was* the same station (which it was, he now knew), then why did it feel so different? The place was still drowned in silence, but it was a silence less dense. A little thinner; a very, very small amount more distilled, like a gallon of paint that had had a drop of water added to it.

Suddenly Alan thought of something, something so chilling that in an instant he found himself frozen right where he stood.

What if, he thought, a cold shiver running up his spine. *What if someone else has been here?*

That thought shook him terribly. Shivering from more than just the chill of winter, he pulled his sweater taut against his body and gave the place a good, hard look.

Nothing out of place. Nothing at all. In fact, everything seemed a little *too* in place. Unnatural. As though someone had knocked something over and, instead of simply returning it to its original spot in a general way, had gone through the trouble of replacing it right down to its molecular coordinates.

Alan shook his head. No. He was being stupid. Of course no one else had been here. Certainly not some murderer, as he was imagining. The man had already said he was busy; there was no way he had time to pay a visit to some decrepit old train station.

It was a thought Alan came up with on the fly, but it did have a hefty amount of logic to it, and he found himself feeling a little better. Without a doubt, he was the only person here...

A thought struck him. He gulped, and without him willing it, his eyes drifted toward the restrooms.

Correction. He was the only *living* person here.

Alan did not allow his mind to linger on the thought for more than a couple of seconds. He blinked, turned aside, and made his brisk way over to the line of payphones.

He heaved open the booth's door with its usual ear-splitting creak, stepped inside, and allowed the door to groan back into place.

Alan eyed the phone for a long, silent moment, as though he was paying his respects to some long gone ancestors. Then, suddenly, he reached for the phone. He began punching in the number.

But then, something curious happened. The further along he got, the more his hands slowed down. The moment he had arrived at the final number, he froze altogether.

Alan stood gazing at nothing in particular for a good length of time. And though he was reluctant to admit it, he knew what was happening here: He was scared. Scared that it was not all a big coincidence, that he was, at best, a conspirator, at worst an accomplice.

But still, he decided, the truth of the matter needed to be known. So he placed the phone onto the receiver, picked it back up, and then dialed the number, leaving out the stutters and pauses.

It rang, of course. For a reason that eluded him, that only added to his anxiety. After the third ring, the anxious weight in his chest began to lift. He waited, waited, waited... Every passing second of silence was pleasant, almost therapeutic.

Two minutes passed—he'd been counting—and the anxiety drained away entirely. There was not going to be an answer. Realizing the fact, Alan began to smile, feeling awfully lighthearted. That was fine by him:

He'd done his part. It seemed, however, as though the man, fresh out of prison, truly *was* busy; any answers would (*unfortunately*, he thought, not at all honestly) have to wait until Christmas.

Chapter 6

Dusk had fallen. The winter's uncompromising draughts chilled Alan in layers. It seeped into his skin the way ink would seep into a piece of paper: slow but eventual.

Then the chill met his muscles, sending them squeezing in on themselves like a piece of wet cloth being wrung.

And then, once these two great barriers had been traversed, the cold at last was sent to meet Alan's bones, into which it bit and grit and crackled its way.

And through all that, Alan still had the phone pressed against his ear, an idiotic smile on his face. He felt accomplished, thinking that he had overdone himself by attempting to call the murderer for this long.

No answer! He rejoiced in his head. *There's no answer! I've done my end of the deal, now it's not my problem anymore!*

Of course, if he had allowed his mental faculties the opportunity to assess the situation a little more closely, he'd have realized he hadn't *really* been trying all that hard; see, rather than calling in an even spread, say, every two minutes, Alan had kept to the same one call he had made when he arrived, just leaving it to ring and ring. Had his call gone to voicemail, and if the murderer decided to give it a listen, it would simply be dead silence.

Not realizing this, however, Alan at last drew the phone away feeling as happy as could be. His ear beneath was sore and throbbing, the skin of it as red as if it were bleeding.

How long had he been here?

Alan reached forward to place the phone back in place—and was startled to note that he could no longer see where its place *was*. He looked around wildly. Night had fallen at some point, he now realized, but he had known nothing about it.

He reached out and groped around in front of him until he found the hook, upon which he set the telephone.

Alan suddenly felt remarkably clear-headed. As he blinked hard in a futile attempt to get his eyes to adjust to the dark quicker, he allowed his mind to wander. He hadn't gotten an answer from the murderer himself, but that didn't mean he was done just yet. At least for the sake of clearing his conscience, he still needed *an* answer of some sort.

So, what could he do about that? He knew people who worked for the local paper, but, seeing as it had only said that much, and given that these folks would not leave out any known details of any story they put out, Alan had to conclude that their knowledge was as limited as his own.

Then, what about the cops? They wouldn't be open to sharing anything confidential, surely, but at least they'd be able to provide him with an update—*any* update.

Strolling up to the police station was an idea, but Alan discarded it; after his visit the other day, he wasn't sure they'd be particularly thrilled to see him.

And then he had two ideas simultaneously, one fairly brilliant, the other just flat-out stupid.

The first was to visit the hospital. Lie that the man had been a relative and get some insight from the doctors. Hell, with a bit of luck on his side and a bit of carelessness on the hospital's part, he might even get to see the autopsy report. And, best of all, even if they *didn't* believe him to be a relative, and even if they decided not to tell him anything at all, he would probably not draw a terrible amount of suspicion onto himself.

And yet, despite having come up with this perfectly workable idea, Alan Michaels, a man who not too long ago had been touted as a genius by everyone who knew the name, eschewed it in favor of the other idea:

"Why don't we just head to the crime scene?" said Alan, his voice reverberating in his skull, amplified by the walls of the booth.

In the moment, Alan found it to be a remarkably clever idea. The thought that he could get in trouble—that this excursion could possibly backfire—never for a moment dwelled in that once-brilliant mind.

The shapes present in the dark of the station, a minute ago indistinguishable from one another, now fell on his eyes clearly contoured. He shook his arms and legs in an attempt to try and get the cold out, but it had sunken in too deep by then to be budged by such a simple act.

Alan braced himself, pulled his jacket tighter around him, and pushed open the booth's door.

Rather counter-intuitively, it turned out to be colder *in* the booth than out of it. If Alan had paid attention in physics (or whichever discipline it was that oversaw such phenomena), he was sure he would've understood why that was.

Alan shrugged internally, not particularly interested in figuring it out.

"Right, off we go!" he said, rubbing his hands together, a little impatient. If someone who didn't know Alan saw him in that moment, they would've been forgiven for finding him just a *little* suspicious.

And so his journey began, past dark, bare trees and warm, smiling houses. His eyes were aware of the world sailing past. His ears heard it. His nose smelt it. But his legs, the ones carrying him through this? No, they knew nothing of this little trip—such was the terrific degree to which the cold had put them to sleep.

Well, anyway. Walk, walk, walk, and then he had arrived at the neighborhood in which the murder had taken place.

Alan looked around. Two rows of street lights flanked the wide street, painting the ground a pleasant amber, giving off an air of homely warmth.

Without much thought, Alan strolled up a random driveway and knocked twice on the door that lay at its end. There was a moment of scrambling beyond the door. A moment later it came open, and Alan stood face to face with a young blonde woman.

"Evening, Miss," he said. Then he paused. His expression changed as though he were deep in thought, but in truth it was just the opposite: His mind had gone blank.

"Yes?" the woman said.

Alan scratched the back of his head. Now that he thought about it, he wasn't quite sure how to say, "*Hey! Some guy died around here, I heard, and now I'm trying to invade his home. Would you mind telling me where it is?*" without coming off as a bit of a nut job.

"Well, see," he began, looking at his feet. "I had a friend who used to live in this neighborhood. Loud guy. Said and did as he pleased, never cared what people thought about it." Alan paused to heave a dramatic sigh, then continued slowly, the tiniest of quivers in his voice. "I heard that something happened to him. Something bad." He looked up and peered right into the woman's eyes.

Two sets of eyes remained locked on one another, one drowned in feigned hurt, the other in genuine pity.

The woman opened her mouth, causing Alan's heart to skip a beat. Here it comes; she was about to tell him the address!

"Alan?" she said.

"What?" Alan said sharply, forgetting in an instant all about his act.

"You're talking about Alan, right? Guy with pink hair, pretty short?"

"His name's Alan?" he croaked.

The woman narrowed her eyes. She had been all the way out of her front door a moment ago, but now she took a furtive step back inside, just enough so she could slam the door shut if necessary.

"You say he's your friend, but you don't even know his name?" she questioned, her tone suspicious.

Alan panicked and, unsure why, raised his left hand—she gasped. His heart jumped; both their eyes fell on the same thing: his scars. At once he knew how to get out of this situation.

"Miss," he said, "I was involved in an accident not too long ago. Hasn't even been a year, in fact." He nodded at his hand. "What you see here, believe me, it's nothing compared to what happened inside my head. I suffered pretty bad memory loss, and some of it still hasn't come back."

"O-Oh," the woman stammered, seeming a little taken aback. She shook her head, then asked, "So, what happened to him exactly?"

"Huh?" For a moment he was dumbfounded. "What do you mean, what happened? It was on the news. You mean no one told you?"

"No, I haven't heard anything," she said. She paused for a long while, perhaps hoping for Alan to fill her in. But he didn't, so she sighed and pointed down the street. "Turn left at the intersection, and you'll see a place with a couple of mini topiaries out front. That's the house you're looking for. It's a little way's walk—past the fence and some way down a wooded driveway. Also, it's kind of hidden; Alan liked his privacy. But still, the place is just out there on its own, so as long as you keep an eye out, you shouldn't miss it."

"Alright, thank you," Alan said, and by the time he had reached the "you", he was already a dozen feet down her driveway.

For all the talk she had given about it being hard to find, Alan thought it was... well, right there. The topiaries were of a bear and a wolf, flanking the opulent mahogany door like guards.

No police tape? Alan thought. It was odd, to be sure. Did they *want* their precious evidence to be tampered with?

Alan strolled up the garden-flanked driveway and planted a pair of hard knocks on the door, to no reply. He moved over to the window and tried again. Nothing. Then he tried wrenching the window open, and once that failed, he moved back to the door and jiggled the knob hopelessly.

Once all the conventional attempts at entering proved futile, Alan squatted at the front door and picked up the mat—and the key underneath began to glisten a fiery scarlet from the touch of a streetlight not too far off. Alan sighed; a murderer was on the loose, and folks were still sleeping sound with their keys under the mat. It was ridiculous.

Key in lock. Turn. *Click.*

As simple as that, he was in. He shut the door behind him as gently as if he were placing his own child down in a bed of nails; he was not clued in as to whether the man had lived alone, so stealth was his safest bet. If he were caught breaking and entering into the scene of a crime, his lousy book would be the least of his problems.

All around it was pitch black. He felt around the walls until he found a panel with a great many switches. His thought process at that point was both highly efficient and alarmingly primitive: *No idea what does what, so may as well turn them all on, no?* And turn them all on he did.

One by one lights flickered on and fans whirred to life. The room he was in took a while to receive its share of illumination, but it came eventually. It was, unsurprisingly, the living room. Not terribly large, but very comfortable, with lots of couches and footstools, along with a couple of bean bags in the corners.

The right-hand wall had an arch nearly the width of the wall itself carved into it, leading into the dining area. At the other end of this area, Alan saw another, more normal arch leading into the kitchen.

The stairs were directly to his left, and within a second of the lights coming on, he found his feet carrying him on up. The murder had happened, if memory served right, on the *first* floor, so he wasn't quite sure why his instincts guided him *away* from that very floor.

But he knew better than to distrust his instincts, so up he went.

The hallway up here was a narrow one, hardly enough for two to walk abreast.

There were only three doors up here, two set into the left-hand side of the hallway, the other on the right-hand side. The other end of the hallway was a dead end, dark and adorned with cobwebs in the corners.

The little pocket of space before the dead end was not large, by any means. In fact, many would be hard-pressed to fit anything at all worthwhile in there.

And yet, something within that little space *did* capture his attention. Captured it, and refused to let go. *Odd*, Alan thought. It was something perfectly normal, just sitting there, minding its own business... But the *way* it was sitting, Alan found terribly eerie—it was a phone.

He shook his head and turned away from the phone. He made for the first door (it was on the right) and enclosed his suddenly sweaty hand around the knob.

The door came open. Alan turned on the light, and as it flickered and faltered he imagined he saw something on the bed. Something terrible... mangled... staring...

And then the light came and stayed, revealing to him the room he stood in. The perfectly normal room. Bare apart from a single bed, its covers and pillows, a chairless study in the corner, and a small cupboard opposite the bed.

Alan stepped inside, and the door closed on its own behind him, causing him to turn. He started terribly, his breath catching in his throat.

There was someone behind the door.

Alan froze.

So did the man.

They stared, and stared, and stared, and Alan thawed himself a little.

So did the man.

Alan waved his arms wildly about as though attempting to impersonate insanity.

And so did the man.

"Idiots," Alan muttered. "Has no one told you not to put mirrors behind doors?"

Alan eyed his reflection a moment longer, clicked off the lights, then stepped back outside. He ventured over to the second room.

Click.

It was an exact copy of the first room, except for one thing—a mannequin hand.

Click.

Off to the third room. The curtains in this room were drawn, and thanks to the streetlight that stood smiling in from hardly a dozen feet off, there was no need at all to turn on the lights.

And again, it was the same as the first room, except for another thing: a mannequin's *foot* this time.

Now, why on Earth, Alan thought to himself, *would anyone leave mannequin parts on the study?*

Alan didn't want to think about it, and he checked off this floor as a completed expedition.

Tap, tap, tap said his feet to the stairs as he made his way back down. He briefly eyed both the dining area and kitchen, but there was nothing in either worth making note of. The living room? He dug, and dug, and found nothing there either.

Hallway to the left. Two rooms. Into both he went with nothing, and out of both he came with the same.

And with that, his procrastination was forced to an end. Only one room left. Right at the end of this hallway. The bathroom.

Alan stood outside the door and gulped. He imagined that he smelt something musty... *Rotten.* The smell of death. The same as the one that was present in the bathroom of the old station. But it was just that: his own imagination.

Alan clicked on the lights and watched as they flickered to life around the edges of the door. He placed his hand on the knob. For something made entirely of steel, it felt oddly warm. Like someone had been holding it while he was upstairs, warming it up for this exact moment...

Alan turned it. There was a sharp creak. And then...

Red.

Lots of red. On the floor, dried, and a little on the wall by the sink.

But that was it. No body. No equipment. No prints. Just a big pool of dried blood. The murderer had said that he had planted blood, and not actually done the kill there...

Alan shook his head. *No. It was a coincidence. This murder has nothing to do with that man. He was given a tip, at best.*

And that was when Alan had the idea. The most ridiculous idea he's had so far.

A tip, huh?

Chapter 7

Alan stepped backward out of the bathroom, shut the door, clicked off all the lights on the first floor, then headed upstairs.

The phone at the end of the hallway remained as it had been, lying lazily upon its back, gazing up at the ceiling as if it were a sky full of stars.

Alan's eyes fell on this as soon as he reached the top of the stairs, and he stumbled, overcome by a sudden pang of nervous excitement. He made his way toward it in slow, noiseless steps, as though he were afraid he might wake it if his approach were any louder.

He reached the phone sitting upon a circular, layered table. For a long while he simply gazed at it, a storm of questions assaulting him, sending his thoughts into a frenzy. He shook his head in an attempt to organize himself, and in the process a single question untangled itself from the bunch and cascaded on down. The question was, quite simply, this:

Why is it off of its receiver?

Alan drew his sweater over his fingers and picked up the phone. He pressed it to his ear. Nothing. He set it back on its receiver, picked it up. Now there was a dial tone along with a constant crackle, like paper being crumpled.

Alright. That meant it was working the way phones were *meant* to work. And then his fingers got to work, dialing out his intended number. It was a job much quicker than usual, and the reason for it was simply because the number itself was shorter than usual. Only three digits, in fact.

He finished dialing the number, leaned against the wall behind him, and waited for the operator to connect him to 9-1-1. It was well into the fourth ring when the call was answered.

"Nine one one, what is your emergency?" said the man on the other end, his voice bloated and distorted.

Alan cleared his throat and put on a bit of a high-pitched voice to try and conceal his identity. "Hello. I'm at the scene of the murder."

There was a short pause. "I'm sorry, sir, I don't think I follow."

Alan felt close to giggling, as though he were a child watching someone about to fall for a tiny pitfall he had dug up.

"Like I said, I'm at the scene of the murder."

"Sir, are you currently safe? Is anyone else there with you?"

"No, I'm alone here."

"Sir, please remain calm and remain on the line." The operator allowed a short pause. Alan suspected that the man thought he needed the time to recollect. "Sir, is this a crime in progress? Can you verify that the perpetrator is no longer in the vicinity?"

"No. No, on both," Alan said, starting to feel just a little confused himself. "This was a murder that happened yesterday. There's no body, nothing. Just a big pool of dried blood on the floor." This time Alan was the one who perpetrated a short bout of silence. "It was in the paper. I saw it with my own eyes. How is it that you don't know about it? Hell, they said the autopsy was delayed, which means they *have* the body, just that there's something about it that confuses them. Who would've delivered that body from the crime scene to the hospital if not for you guys?"

"Sir, I can assure you, we haven't collected any cadavers recently." Again there was a pause, only this time it was longer. "Can you please verify something for me? Is there any tape, or any sort of obstruction on the perimeter of the scene?"

"Hmm? Oh, no, there isn't," Alan said. "I found that a little irresponsible, too. What if the evidence gets tampered with?"

"Sir, as a possible witness, I'm going to have to ask you a few questions." Alan heard the rustling and flipping of paper—in this day and age, was this man really about to handwrite a report instead of simply typing it out?

"Mhmm. No problem. Except," Alan said, a sly grin appearing on his face, "I'm not a witness. Not at all."

Pause. "I don't follow," said the operator.

"I was given a tip, is all." The moment those words left his mouth, Alan felt an odd feeling of power. He, quite possibly, knew something that the police themselves were not privy to. Again, Alan wasn't quite sure *how* that could've been, considering it had been printed in mass by the local press, and that they must've wrung the details from *someone*. Did Alan care about this at all? No, not quite. All he knew was that he was in the know, and buddy on the line was not.

"Who was it that tipped you off, sir?"

"Well..." Alan said, trying to force his tone into something mysterious. "I just know a guy. I had nothing to do with the murder, though, I can assure you."

"Sir, you can leave that up for us to decide. Now, I'd like to know a few things. I'd appreciate it if you cooperated." The scratch of a pencil on paper—not even a pen, just a plain ol' graphite pencil—dominated the line for approximately five seconds. "Alright, sir, can I get your exact location and your name?"

Alan remained silent, his heart pounding but a wide grin on his face. His eyes were not cued in, however, and they opted to remain slack and emotionless, causing his expression to give off a distinct air of insanity.

"Sir? If you are still on the line, please respond," the operator said.

"I'm still here, yes."

"I'm going to need an answer, sir. I repeat: What is your current location, and what is your full name?"

"My current location..." Alan trailed off. "My current location is the scene of the crime. And my name's a secret."

"Sir, if you keep playing these games, I'm going to have to assume your presence at this supposed crime scene is, at best, a combination of breaking and entering and obstruction of justice."

"Obstruction of justice? How so? Also, I'd hardly call it *breaking* and entering if the guy had his front door key under the damn mat."

"Obstruction of justice constitutes tampering with or destroying evidence, refusal to—"

"I didn't tamper with anything," Alan said, genuinely annoyed by that accusation. Just look, he was touching things with his jacket and not his fingers, all to avoid leaving prints. Hell, he was even wearing one of those ridiculous baseball caps to keep his hair from falling all over the place.

"Sir, this murder you're talking about, it happened in a house?"

"Yes."

"And this call is being made through the same house's land-line, is that correct?"

"It is, yes."

"Sir, whether inadvertent or not, that constitutes tampering with evidence. If not tampering, then contamination at the very least."

"Ah, I see." There was a pause, a pause so long that Alan wouldn't have been surprised if the sun began to peek over the horizon.

There was a sharp crackle on the line, then the operator spoke. "Sir, I'm sure you are aware, but I'd like to remind you that we can pinpoint your location based on the land-line you're calling from."

"That's not a problem. Even if you send people over, what could you charge me with? Other than maybe unlawful entry."

"If nothing else, if this turns out to be a baseless call and there's no real crime, we can charge for misdemeanor in the form of a prank call."

There was the scratching once again, and it went on and on for nearly an entire minute. Alan couldn't help but feel a little curious as to what it was he was writing.

"Sir, can I get your full name?"

Alan's heart gave a leap, but it was more out of excitement than fear.

He didn't ask for my location this time. Does that mean he knows where I am?

"Sir, are you still on the line?"

"Yes, yes. Hold on," he said impatiently.

"It shouldn't take this long for you to tell me your name," the operator said.

Alan chuckled; he'd just thought of a new way of toying with these people. "You want my name, yes? Well, it's the same."

The operator paused, and Alan knew exactly why: He assumed Alan had more to say. After a good few seconds in which Alan made it glaringly obvious that he did not have anything to add, the operator spoke.

"I don't follow, sir."

"The victim's name. You asked for it, I'm telling it: It's the same."

"The same as what?"

"The same as mine."

There was a short pause, then a short spell of scratching. "You mean to tell me that you and the victim share a name?"

"Yes."

"Sir, I have to ask. Is this by any chance some extremely roundabout attempt at reaching out for help?"

Alan laughed. "No, no. I'm fine. Well, not *fine,* per se, but not quite suicidal, as you're implying. I meant what I said. This dead man and I happen to share a name. Pure coincidence. Nothing more to it than that."

"Sir, regardless, I'm going to have to ask you to stay on the line. Your statement as a witness is extremely valuable."

"I told you, I'm not a witness. I didn't witness anything."

"You said you were tipped off," said the operator. "Regardless of whether it's as a witness or not, you seem to be privy to information that we aren't. That information could help us solve this case."

Alan laughed. He was enjoying himself, perhaps more than he should have been.

By this point, if Alan had been in anything resembling a normal mental state, he would've realized the magnitude of what he was doing. It wasn't just stupid, and it wasn't just careless (although both were hefty ingredients in this nonsense soufflé). No, what he was doing was something more: criminal.

The operator spoke once more, and his half-hearted attempt at concealment did not stop Alan from catching the irritation in his voice.

"Sir, is there any particular reason you keep wedging in all these pauses?"

"Ah, no, no. I'm just thinking. Give me a second to think."

"There's no point to all your thinking if you fail to answer my questions anyway," said the operator. "I've already asked twice: What is your full name?"

"I already told you, it's a secret. You shouldn't ask people to reveal their secrets, it's bad manners."

"Can you reveal the name of the person who gave you the tip-off?"

That caused Alan to pause for real. Now he thought about it, he didn't actually know.

"I'm not too sure what his name is, honestly. He's never told me. We've only ever spoken two, three times."

"That's alright, sir. I've dispatched one of our detectives to your location to validate your report, so I request that you do not leave the scene until he arrives. If he determines that a crime had taken place, he will take a statement from you. During the questioning, please remember to remain truthful, as any information you provide can help us solve this case."

Alan felt a cold shiver. *This is it, the grand finale.*

"But," Alan said, putting on an innocent, clueless voice, "why does it need to be *solved?*"

"I don't follow, sir. According to yourself, a murder has taken place. And murders need to be solved so perpetrators can be brought to justice."

"I know that, of course. But that's only in general," said Alan. "*This* case in particular doesn't need any solving."

"Again, I don't follow. Why do you believe that this case sees no need to be solved, sir?"

"Well, that's because it's already been solved." He allowed a short, dramatic pause to settle between them, then said, "I know who the murderer is."

And without waiting a moment longer, he slammed the phone down on the receiver.

In that moment, it was as though an entire lifetime's worth of adrenaline was coursing through his veins. Even during the crash, that singular moment when he knew that a second from now, his life would be over, even *that* did not hold a candle to the rush he felt now.

A small part of him wanted to wait on the detective, see what he had to say. But, he should've counted his lucky stars that all that adrenaline did nothing to cloud his wits. He could see as well as anyone else how bad of an idea that was.

Of course, there was only one other logical course of action: get the hell out.

And yet, the primal, thoughtless part of him, his own personal devil-on-shoulder, whispered only one thing to him: *Stay. It'll make for a good chapter. You're innocent anyway, so why worry?*

He was not an accomplice, of course, and apart from the tip-off he had nothing to do with this. But when the cops arrived as they surely would, and when they knocked him to the ground and threw him in cuffs before asking any questions, then Alan would regret not turning tail.

An idle second took place in which the two halves of Alan decided which course of action to take with a good old fashioned game of tug-of-war. Eventually, the logical part won, and Alan was forced to consent.

Alan double checked all the rooms upstairs, making sure he hadn't bothered anything, clicked off all the lights, and in the pitch black dark went back downstairs. Everything was checked here as well, and once he was certain everything was in place, he crept over to the backdoor (it was unlatched), slipped out, set the door back, and made his quiet escape.

As the woman said, the man's house was a short way into the woods. Alan walked parallel to the driveway's entrance, waiting for a spot that struck onto a familiar path to appear.

He hadn't been walking for two minutes when a distant sound sent a pleasantly anxious shiver down his spine: sirens, long, unrelenting, and, without a doubt, closing in on *Alan's* home.

Chapter 8

The sirens remained blaring in the distance, but they had by now turned into a faint, incoherent pinprick of a sound, hardly a separate entity from the hoots and cricks that dominated the late night air.

Alan smiled to himself, feeling energetic in a tingly sort of way. The cops? They were all the way over there, not a clue in the world where he was. Although, that wasn't particularly surprising, since Alan *himself* had no clue where he was.

Despite the pitch black darkness that had enveloped him back in the woods, he had managed to find his way out. The problem was what came after. He had struck an odd exit and landed himself in a spot he knew nothing about, and he was now attempting to return to the path well-trodden with nothing but streetlights and moonlight for guidance.

It took just short of half an hour, but Alan did eventually manage to find the way back onto familiar territory. He could hear sirens still wailing in the distance—he *thought* he could hear them, at least.

Alan paused, allowing himself a moment of thought, and the conclusion he arrived at was that it simply could not have been so. The noise had been infinitesimal several miles ago, and there was a scarce chance that Alan could still pick up on their sound waves all the way from here.

The very instant he had this thought, the wailing vanished; it had been nothing more than a figment of his imagination, as though his brain, unsure of the exact moment the real noise had faded away, had decided to keep the ghost of it playing in his head.

Alan shook his head. He was discovering more and more facets to his post-accident self as the days went by. It was nice in a way, like a messed up game of hide-and-seek, where his former self was hiding behind rocks and leaves, awaiting the moment they were overturned so they could at last be reunited. Nonetheless, he would be lying if he said it didn't wear him down.

Anyway, here he was, back in the parts of town he was comfortable navigating. It must've been close to eleven at night, but there was still an odd scattering of people about: Over there, a man was smoking under the streetlights, and a little farther up was a family of four huddled around the table outside of a closed café.

A little farther down, Alan came to a certain corner. Nestled in that corner was a quiet little building. It wasn't too long ago that Alan didn't know this place existed. And now he was eyeing that delicatessen the way the pope would look at a Church.

The second his eyes fell on it, the tingly happiness inside of him expanded like a helium balloon. Without him willing it, his walk turned into more of a skip, and all the way home, that was exactly the way it remained.

What a sight it was, that of a middle-aged man skipping the pale evening hours away as though he had not a care in the world. Such a beautiful thing to behold, and yet there was not a soul about at this time to witness it.

Alan's clothes were frosted around the edges, and his bones felt like the deepest, most private part of a glacier, and even that did nothing to dampen his mood. He was feeling exceedingly jovial; had anyone else been around at this time, Alan would've no doubt approached them, and he would've grabbed both their hands and given them a rough, jittery handshake, the type a sycophantic vendor would give a customer.

The fact that he was so elated was surprising, even to himself. He had just pulled a prank that could quite easily land him in prison if they managed to track him down. And, of course, they would, seeing as, in his own roundabout way, he had let the cops know his name. But still, he didn't care, and all the way home he skipped like a rabbit that'd had a little too much coffee.

His skip lasted *most* of the way home, but it fell just short of the *whole* way. Just around the corner of his street he stumbled and paused, and at that moment his light skipping turned into a plain walk. The reason for it was simple: At what must've been half past midnight, his wife was standing outside their door, watching him as he approached, her eyes a mixture of emotions he couldn't quite place.

Her arms were crossed in front of her chest, and she was leaning against the doorway, lending her overall posture an air of boredom. It seemed familiar to Alan; he was sure she'd subjected him to it before, but he wasn't quite sure when.

"Nala?" he said the moment he reached the end of their driveway. "Why aren't you in bed? Didn't you read what was in the paper? You shouldn't be out this late, it's dangerous. What if someone does something to you?"

It was a long-winded series of questions, to be sure, but it did not hold a candle to what Nala had to say.

"Do you know what time it is, Alan?"

More than anything else, her tone surprised him. It was an uneven blend of two emotions. The first was worry, and it made up most of her tone. This was not surprising. The other emotion, despite being present in such a small proportion, somehow stood at the foreground of her voice; if someone else had heard her in that moment, they would've hardly guessed that she was worried. This other emotion was fear. Alan had no clue why it was there.

Never for a moment did Alan think that was all she had to say, and he didn't need to wait long to be proven right.

"Do you have any idea how worried I've been? You said you were going to go write, so I thought you'd be fine. You weren't back by, what, seven? I got worried, so I went to check at that diner. You weren't there. I asked the owner and she said you'd been there since the early morning all the way into the evening. She said someone came in with the papers, you bought one, then rushed out of the place. I went asking around but no one had seen you. That was, oh, I don't know, four, five hours ago. It's close to twelve-thirty in the morning, Alan. Do you have any clue how stressed I've been over here? I even considered going and filing a missing person report, but I held myself back because I was sure you'd know how to take care of yourself. If you'd have taken a single hour longer to get back, though, you could bet that I'd have begged them to get a search team out. You've been out all day, you know. You didn't even leave me a note. Not even a note, and you're asking me why *I'm* not in bed yet? Well, how d'you expect me to—"

"Jesus, Nala!" Alan said, wondering to himself where exactly she found the lung capacity to orchestrate these rants. "I'm not a kid. I'm allowed to stay out late if I want."

"I never said you couldn't," she snapped. "But at least tell me first. Also, on the topic of what we are and aren't allowed to do, in case you haven't noticed, I'm your *wife*. I'm allowed to worry about your well-being. You can't pretend *you* wouldn't be worried if you didn't know where I was and I wasn't back even past midnight."

Alan thought about this.

"Yeah, I would be worried. But I wouldn't make such a big deal out of it."

"Alan, you would. Don't pretend."

The pair eyed each other for a long moment. The air between them was not exactly hostile, but it was only a step or two down from it. One misplaced comment and it would get there.

It was Nala who spoke first, and it was only after a long, long while of staring.

"For now, why don't you just come on in?" She rubbed the cuff of his sweater between her fingers, sending flakes of unseen frost spiraling to the ground. "Winter's here, more or less. I don't really care where you were all this time, so long as you're safe now. Wherever you were, though, it must have been freezing."

She turned aside, making for the stairs. Alan turned off all the lights on the first floor—the action excited him, for it reminded him of the stunt he'd just pulled—and then stepped onto the landing to follow Nala. "Take off your clothes and go warm yourself up with a bath. Your skin is ice cold."

And he did. While she was in the bathroom, Alan began to think. More specifically, he was thinking about that little bit of fear her voice had held... In fact, no, he was not thinking. He *had* been thinking, ever since he'd returned. But now no more; now he was concluding. And his conclusion was this: Nala knew something was amiss. Of course, there was no chance of her guessing right—in fact, if she *did* guess right, he'd be a little offended; what he was doing *was* tasteless, but for her to *guess* it? That was just disrespectful, and Alan would be forced to reconsider his wife's perception of him.

No, she didn't know exactly what it was that he was doing. But the problem was, she was in the ballpark. He could tell. Tell that her frustration at him stemmed not from *not* knowing, but from *half* knowing.

There was nothing to be gained from prolonging this whole ordeal. He'd have to find a way to smooth away her doubts. And if the way of doing it involved a few lies, then so be it. Was he a fan of lying to his wife? No, not quite. But when the book came out and he shot into stardom overnight, then she'd know.

"Nala," Alan said. "I can tell you're suspicious. I don't get why. Do you think I'm cheating on you or something?"

Nala made a noise that sounded close to a choke, her eyes going as wide as a cat's in a pair of headlights. She seemed terribly taken aback by the suggestion.

"No, of course not!" she said, her voice going a little squeaky in her surprise. "I didn't once think that! I'm worried about your safety, not your—your—your chastity!" She glared at him, a look of mild hurt apparent in her eyes. "Please, never suggest something like that again, Alan. Do you see me as someone who just blindly jumps to the worst possible conclusion, not a second thought about it?" *Worst possible conclusion, eh?* thought Alan. Oh, she didn't know the half of it. Didn't know that the honest truth was far worse. "Do you think of me as that sort of woman? Huh, Alan?"

"No, Nala, I didn't really think that you thought that way," said Alan.

And it was true enough. He'd said it as nothing more than a red herring; just in case she had been on course to the right answer, he wanted to force a detour, even if only for a little while. Alan had not expected her to react so strongly, but apart from that, the distraction seemed to have done its job.

"Then what, Alan? Why would you suggest that, then? Do you know how badly things like that hurt me?"

He heaved a long, dramatic sigh. Quite the performance Alan Michaels was putting on, if he did say so himself. "Now, let's forget about it. We can discuss it another day, but for now, I'm pretty sure the both of us are way too worn out for such nonsense."

Nala's face went tight, and a moment later she relaxed. She smiled for the first time that day, and Alan was wholeheartedly happy to see it.

"I'll make you a deal, Alan," Nala said. "Instead of discussing it another day, what's say we don't bring it back up at all?" Her voice was playful in the most childish way, and Alan was struck by a sudden, unbearable pang of love for her.

He smiled back at her. "Alright, let's."

"But!" said Nala. "Alan, you have to promise me. Never make me worry like that again. If you want to stay out, leave a note preemptively. I'll do the same, of course."

Alan smiled. "I promise."

Nala smiled back at him, then suddenly shifted her eyes. Her smile slipped off of her face, and she fidgeted. She began twirling her hair with her fingers. Alan knew what this was well enough: something was eating her up.

"Um, Alan..." She fidgeted, glanced at him, flung her eyes away, sighed, and forced herself to stare at him head on. "Listen. I want to be completely honest with you. When you didn't come home, I thought you had... You know, gotten tempted. I was afraid you'd done something stupid, something you'd regret."

Alan's heart skipped a beat. That description was a little too close to the mark. Only, he was not regretting anything. He suspected, however, that a fresh day would change that.

"What kind of something?" Alan asked, trying hard to seem casual, but inadvertently averting his gaze midway. If Nala had noticed, she made nothing of it.

"You know, just... stuff. I know you avoid the topic like the plague, so I'm sorry for bringing it up. I just think I need to be completely honest with my feelings."

"No, that's good, Nala. But you don't need to worry about me. Really. To tell you the truth, I've been really struggling with my writing. I've had a few general ideas I've been fleshing out, but I haven't actually *written* anything. Not yet. I just thought I needed a change of scenery, a fresh perspective, you know. I went wandering, and I guess I got a little carried away."

"A *little* carried away?" Nala said, putting on a stern face and crossing her arms in front of her chest.

Alan scratched the back of his neck. "Okay, a lot carried away."

The two eyed each other for a short moment. There was no hostility now. Just a husband and a wife, perfectly in love with each other, just the way God intended. The latter broke into a wide grin, and she stumbled into her husband's arms. In an instant she was on her tiptoes, her chin rested on his shoulder.

"Alan, I know you've changed. I'm sorry for jumping to conclusions."

She gave him a peck on the cheek, which was quite the struggle considering she was an entire head shorter than him. But Alan hardly noticed. He was busy thinking about what she'd just said.

She knows I've changed? From what?

"Now, Alan, I think it's about time you went and took your bath. Maybe it'll help you get some ideas."

A perfectly reasonable suggestion. He went over to the bathroom door, got his towel from off its hook, and slipped on inside. The tub was still steaming, and as he sank into it, it felt as though the chill and languor and numbness the day had infused into him were washed away in an instant.

But his heart? Oh, his heart was certainly *not* relaxed. Not one bit. It was hammering in his chest in such devastating thumps that it seemed to scare his lungs, slicing his breaths into thin and shallow strips.

It had nothing to do with the sudden temperature change his body was forced to undergo. Neither yet was it related to the earlier events of the day. It wasn't even the massive spider behind the door that Nala had somehow missed.

No. This hammering was simply the result of his shame. Despite his earlier thought that he was willing to slip in a few lies to get her off his back, he now felt terrible that he'd actually done it.

Alan sighed and rested an elbow on the edge of the tub. He couldn't do a thing about what had already been done, so no point mulling over it.

Alan watched the spider. It had managed to sneak itself halfway out of the top edge of the door. Alan found himself hoping that it found a way to get its *whole* self on the outside. Just so he could get the damn thing off his back.

Chapter 9

The grand, primordial entity that measly humans called the universe had several laws its Creator had set in place before allowing it to touch the canvas of existence: nothing with mass could travel beyond the speed of light; everything out there, no matter how long from now, had an expiration date; and Nala Michaels absolutely did not awaken before her husband.

On one jolly morning on a little blue-green planet, one of these rules was broken.

Alan woke to the sun in his eyes. Imagine his shock; he was usually up while the sky outside was still pale, and by the time the sun was peeking over the horizon, he would've found himself in a certain diner crunching away at a slice of toast.

Alan groaned. Without opening his eyes he got out of bed, drew the curtains shut, got back in bed, and turned onto his side. He slapped the other side of the bed, but no matter how much he did, all that met his fingers were crumpled sheets and wrinkled blankets. Certainly nothing that could've been his wife.

"Nala?" Alan called.

Radio silence.

"Hello, Nala?" he repeated, a little louder this time. A bird upon the windowsill seemed to think the cry was meant for it, and so it began chirping away in its glee.

That was the only reply his call received, and since Alan was quite sure his wife was not a bird, he opened his eyes.

Nala's side of the bed was empty. The bedsheets had come undone at one corner, her pillow had slipped out of its case, and her blanket lay crumpled upon the bed.

Alan sighed for two reasons. The first, he had overslept so badly that Nala had woken before him. And the second, he was mildly annoyed at her; he knew she was a thrasher, but she could've done her side of the bed at least. When he woke first (which was all the time, just to be clear), he always did his side.

There was another reason he was annoyed, but it was a more general sort of annoyance, not directed at something or someone in particular. He tended to make full use of the fact that he woke first by sneaking out without having to inform anyone. But now with Nala up, he'd have to run into her at least once. Bottom line: there would be no sneaking out for him today.

Alan took off his clothes, stepped into the shower, wet himself, turned the water off, and lathered his wet hair in shampoo. A navy shower, as they called it.

All lathered up, Alan turned the shower back on, and as its warmth enveloped him and chased away the cold in his flesh and bones, he began to lament.

What a horrible day to have woken late. Why? Well, just look. The cone-shaped pines stood proud at the front of every home on his street, each spiraled with running lights and strewn with baubles and candy canes and miniature snowmen.

But it didn't stop there. Alan turned the shower off, and in the silence he heard it: the distinct sound of carols, small and far away, but nonetheless infusing a remarkable jolliness in anyone who cared to listen.

That's right. It was the morning of Christmas—X-mas, if you will. The day Alan was supposed to run down to the old station and have his scheduled interview with his murderous pal.

Well, he thought as he stepped into a set of warm clothes. *Maybe Nala won't mind me leaving if it's only for a bit.*

Nala was at the table, sipping away at something while the radio filled the air with Christmas music.

As Alan came down the stairs, the *tap, tap* of his feet on the wooden floorboards alerted her to his presence. She turned to him, and at once she narrowed her eyes.

"Why are you dressed so warmly?" she asked. If she was trying to keep her suspicion out of her voice, she was failing rather badly.

Alan was taken aback. Had she always been this perceptive? Regardless, he managed to mask his surprise in an expression of polite confusion.

"What are you talking about, Nala? It's a white Christmas, of course I'm dressed warmly. Everyone is."

"But you're not weak to the cold, are you? I've seen you make snow angels shirtless back when you were younger." She allowed a moment of silence to settle between them. She took a sip of her drink, then said, "Were you planning on going anywhere today?"

"Well, not exactly, no." There were still six hours between him and his talk. May as well try and appease her for now, pretend something urgent came up later.

Nala made a face that said she didn't believe him. "That's good. Do you remember, Alan? The promise we made all those years ago, back when the kids had just moved out? That Christmas was a day meant for family—if the kids aren't here, then fine. We can make it a day for just the two of us. We promised, just for one day, we wouldn't let anything get between us."

"Of course I remember." He did not. "Like I said, I'm not planning on going anywhere, Nala. I'm dressed this way because it's cold, that's all."

They looked at each other, and he could see the suspicion draining from her eyes, bit by bit. She broke into a wide grin.

"That's good. I'm just reminding is all. It's been a while, right?" *Been a while since what?* he thought. And a thought it remained, for she continued before he could get it out. "Anyway, for today, just forget about your writing. I know you feel bad that you haven't started, but it's not good to let it weigh you down."

Alan nodded, feeling more than a little mystified. It had been nearly a month since he'd gone out, or otherwise even mentioned his writing. It was odd that she'd bring it up all of a sudden, but it was even more odd that she was right. She had managed to hit the bull's-eye twice without being given a single arrow, and how she had done it was beyond him.

Well, Alan thought. *Worst case scenario, I slip off while she's in the bathroom, and I say someone had called for something urgent.*

He was prepared to kneel and beg for forgiveness, for he knew he'd get it. For now, though, his date with the death dealer was more important.

And so for the rest of the day, Alan waited for an opportunity, for just the tiniest of windows to present itself, and he'd be on his way.

It never came.

Nala, despite having said that her words were nothing more than a reminder, kept a very close eye on him. She seemed certain—*oddly* certain—that he was not being truthful, that he had every intention of going out. Almost as if she'd gotten a tip-off.

Alan would glance at a door, turn back, and Nala would be eyeing him, suspicion in her eyes but never a word leaving her lips. He got up and went somewhere, she'd tail him, pretending she had something do in the same room. It happened again, and again, and again...

By the time the hour hand had risen to the twelve, Alan began to feel more than a little annoyed. By the time it found its way to the one, he was downright sick. Why did she think it was necessary to scrutinize him this way? Did she not trust him?

And then, at last, the hour hand landed on the two. The scheduled time was here, and the payphones were miles away. Alan glanced at the clock and sighed. He no longer felt annoyed by Nala's antics. He understood. She just wanted them to be together.

For the rest of the day, despite the promised time having elapsed, Alan still hazarded a few half-hearted attempts at sneaking out. His desire to leave had ebbed, but Nala's desire not to let him remained wholly intact.

Seven in the evening. The sky had gone dark, dinner had been set on the table, and Alan had probably been added to a certain man's list. Perhaps a week from now the murderer would be telling some other hopeless writer the story of this middle-aged, balding man he'd done away with.

"Alan, why aren't you eating?" Nala asked. "In this kind of weather, you can't expect your food to stay warm for too long." She pushed his plate a little closer before setting herself on the chair opposite him.

"Yes, yes, I know," said Alan. He picked up his knife and fork, tore out a chunk of the turkey leg on his plate, and had almost managed to get it into his mouth—when there was a great knock on the door.

Hysteria. Such a powerful word, and yet it did not come close to describing Alan's reaction.

Alan shot up from his chair in a terrible panic—whoever was outside that door, he did not want to meet them. The tablecloth snagged on his sweater's zipper, and down went their entire dinner, crashing to the ground.

Nala gave a startled gasp, but Alan did not notice. He stumbled and sent his chair to the ground with a crash, stepped on the china plates and mugs, sending them splintering into infinitesimal shards and cutting his soles in the process, tripped and crashed into the bathroom door, and nearly tore the very same door off of its hinges in his desperation to wrench it open. He shut it behind him with a boom like dynamite exploding in a quarry, and, panting, slid down against the door into a sitting position.

He was seeing stars, and his temples and eyes were throbbing. He heard the front door open, and Nala's gasp came a second later. Slowly his breathing settled, and Alan set the back of his head against the door and looked upwards, almost as though in prayer.

Nala was out there talking. He could hear her voice, how uncomfortable she sounded. It was a second before his brain processed the other two voices. Both male, both well-spoken, and both with an air of command about them.

Alan recognized one of the voices; it was the man who had been gazing into the display by the delicatessen all those weeks ago. The cop who had been speaking on the phone... The cop Alan had so desperately avoided.

And now here he was at Alan's doorstep, probably another cop buddy with him.

Nala was fidgeting. He couldn't see her, and there was no way he could've known this, but he knew, without a shadow of a doubt. What a mess Alan felt, hiding in the bathroom while his bite-sized wife braved the two massive men at the door.

Several minutes passed, and the conversation outside seemed like it was not close to wrapping up any time soon. Alan was now calm enough to think at least marginally straight. He wondered if he dared eavesdrop on the conversation—if his own name came up on a single occasion, he was certain he'd suffer a cardiac arrest.

At last, after several minutes of wondering, Alan decided to do it. He had to know what these folks had to say, or he'd never be able to rest easy again. So he pressed his ear to the door. Nala's voice fell on his ears, muffled and made hollow by the wood of the door.

"Well, did you find out who did it?" asked Nala.

"No, not yet," said one of the cops. "But we have our suspicions. Is your husband around?"

Alan tore away from the door, his freshly-settled heart now hammering again. He had heard enough to know what they were talking about; they had finally found out about the phone call. Even now, stressed as he was, he still couldn't help but wonder how it came to be that the local press had known about a murder before the cops did.

Regardless, it seemed as though Alan's brilliant idea of baiting the cops had now caught up to him.

Alan remained on the floor, his arms embracing his knees. And that was how he remained for a long time, waiting, waiting...

And then, at last, the wonderful sound came: the thud of the front door shutting. He heard the latch click into place, followed by the slapping of feet on the floor making a beeline for the bathroom.

Knock knock knock.

Alan opened the door, a stupid smile plastered on his face. Nala, however, did not find the situation as amusing as he did. Her look was not quite a glare, but it was very close.

"What in the world," she said, stepping aside and gesturing towards the broken plates and spilt gravy and the turkey on the floor, and the general mess the kitchen was in, "is *this?*"

"Um..." he began, failed to find anything to add to it, and dropped his eyes, "I'm really sorry. I don't know what came over me."

Nala sighed. "Alan, I get it. You've been jumpy ever since that accident. There's no shame in that."

"It's not that." Alan's head was in his hands, and his voice was dry and flat.

Nala cocked her head. "What is it, then?"

Alan could only hold his silence, for the truth was something he could never tell Nala: He had thought it was the murderer. It was a fair conclusion in Alan's eyes; he had failed to make good of their promised meet-up, meaning the murderer would be furious, and now there was a knock on the door. The first in years.

"Alan," Nala said, her eyes drowned in pity. "I know the accident made you fear the cops. You're scared they'll take you away, thinking it was your fault. But you have to understand, Alan: You aren't a criminal. They've got no reason to come seeking you out, because you haven't done anything wrong.

Alan nodded along despite not agreeing. At this point, he was certain he would count as a small case criminal, a public nuisance, if nothing else.

"You're right, Nala. I'm sorry."

The two of them went into the kitchen. Despite anything that may have come between them, their housekeeping was a sight to behold, for it was close to choreography. Alan mopped up the gravy, Nala swept up the shards, the pair slinking in and out of gaps the other had left, their bodies coming inches close but never touching.

Alan then threw together a couple of deli lunch meat sandwiches, and the two of them began to eat. Quite the downgrade from an entire stuffed turkey, but, oh well. At least it was something.

And that was that. Or, so Alan thought.

While the two of them were getting ready for bed, he cast a casual glance in the mirror—and in his peripheral he caught Nala's reflection giving him in an odd look. A look he didn't quite understand. He shivered.

"Nala," Alan said, turning to neither her nor her reflection. "Can I ask you something?"

"Mhmm. Go ahead."

"The cops, what were they here for?"

The reply Alan feared most was what he was met with—silence. His heart rate picked up. Just as he was about to ask again, Nala sighed.

"Alan, you're still worried about that? I thought I told you to relax. You haven't done anything wrong."

"Yes, I know," Alan said impatiently. "But I'd still like to know what they said."

"I was getting to it," she said. "Well, long story short, someone was murdered recently. It didn't happen close to us, several miles away, if the cops were right. But, still, they're going door to door of every building in the entire town, warning people to keep their doors and windows locked." Nala gave him an amused look. "They didn't make a beeline for *our* place, specifically, if that's what you were thinking."

"Oh," Alan said.

And this time, that really *was* that.

The carolers were now in the neighborhood, and their song filled him with a joy that was hard to describe. He turned off the lights, and with the carols filling the night air, Alan felt as though a boulder he had been carrying had slipped off of his shoulders. Such a wonderful feeling it was, and it was in such glee that Alan rolled over in bed, lay his head on Nala's arm, and bid her yet another Christmas goodnight.

Chapter 10

There were still a few hours left of the Lord's birthday, and the carolers, the most pious of them, at least, seemed to be in a rush to get in as much caroling as time would allow. They had no interest in the warmth of their hearths and the shelter of their roofs, instead choosing to do what they could to spread the holiday spirit.

It was this merry bunch and their choir that woke Alan. He was now sitting up in bed, waiting for his eyes to adjust to the dark.

At first he had been annoyed at being woken up... but then he thought about it. He'd meant to have his talk with the murderer earlier today, but he couldn't, because Nala had had three eyes on him all day.

But now? Now, Nala was asleep, and given how much energy she'd expended today on cooking and cleaning and dealing with the cops and scrutinizing him, Alan was certain she wouldn't awaken until the sun came peeking in through the gaps in the curtains and threatened to fry her retinas through her eyelids.

What all of this meant was rather simple: Alan could go conduct his interview, take a leisurely stroll halfway home, book a cab the rest of the way, take a shower, get dressed, and climb back in bed without Nala ever knowing he'd been gone.

And so Alan's day began, much earlier than it usually did. He disentangled his arm from under his sleeping wife, slowly got up from the bed, and stretched his arms over his head.

He eyed the bathroom for a moment, wondering if he could afford a shower. In the end he decided against it; he'd be taking one as soon as he got back, so what was the point? He removed his sweater from the hook behind the door, threw it on, held the door ajar, squeezed his way out like a bipedal crab, and shut the door noiselessly behind him.

The living room lay in complete darkness apart from two squares of pale light on the floor, the footprints of the moonlight that leaked in through the windows. Alan reached for the front door, but all of a sudden he remembered something that made his hand stutter to a stop—the front door creaked.

He wasn't sure when it began, but it'd been hell-bent on whistle-blowing on him for a good while now. Well, it wasn't going to win today.

Alan pulled his hand away from the doorknob, then headed for the window. He undid its latch, pushed it open with some difficulty (mounds of snow had pooled on the windowsill), and stepped onto the ledge. For someone halfway through his forties, the amount of dexterity he still possessed was remarkable.

He shifted one leg to the other side, then the other, then jumped lightly onto the carpet of snow outside. And just like that, he was out.

He couldn't put the window's latch back in place from the outside, so he just shut the window as far as it would go and left it.

Alan began to walk down his driveway, allowing himself a big stretch and a yawn.

The sky was pitch black and smudged here and there with the gray of clouds, their little gaps filled with stars twinkling quietly to themselves. There was nothing about the world at present that alluded to a dawn upcoming.

Despite the winter draughts coming in hard and often, they seemed never to touch anything. None of the trees swayed, no snow slipped off of branches, and if there were any animals about, they were not making their presence felt. *Nothing* was making their presence felt. In fact, apart from his own footsteps, there was not a sliver of noise around to disturb the silence.

Alan found it eerie. He tried walking slower in hopes of reducing the sound of his footfalls, but it made no difference. He didn't like this.

Not a single bit. What if someone—some*thing*—heard his footsteps and decided to make straight for him? Or, what if...

Alan shook his head. He had somewhere to be, and, more importantly, somewhere to return to. He had no time to be worrying about his strange, overly vivid imagination. After all, that station was so dark and isolated, if anyone ever wanted to do away with him, they could just do it there and leave the body in plain sight. Nobody with any sense would ever come there to find it, and by the time someone with *no* sense came and discovered him, he'd be nothing more than a skeleton, sitting lonely in that station like its very own mascot.

Actually, Alan thought, throwing his gaze about and being met with near-unanimous darkness, *speaking of that old station, it'll be way too dark to navigate, won't it?*

It was that thought that prompted him to take a little detour.

For the first time in his middle-class life, he paid close attention to the gated communities that he passed. Or, more accurately, he paid attention to the little shacks that stood right next to the automated barriers that allowed entry into said communities.

The first such shack he passed was occupied. Alan passed it by, sparing the guard a quick, non-suspicious smile and a nod, both of which were promptly returned. The same thing happened the second time, then the third.

Only the fourth shack he encountered was empty. He had no clue when the guard would be back, so he would have to be quick. He approached very quietly, no sudden movements, slipped inside, and began rummaging about in boxes and in bags. Nestled deep in the bottom of one box, his fingers found what he was looking for before his eyes did: a flashlight.

He pointed it at the wall of a house and gave it a quick test. Its beam sliced through the darkness and painted the wall such a lurid shade of amber that it startled Alan. He fumbled with the flashlight and hastily turned it off, hoping against hope that nobody noticed that.

Well, on the bright side, now he knew it worked. He did a quick, sloppy job of setting the boxes and bags where they had been, then slipped out just as quietly as he had slipped in.

The rest of the walk to the station was as peaceful as could be. It was silent, but no longer to the point that it was eerie. It was punctuated here and there with a hoot or crick, or a mound of snow slipping off of a bough and crashing to the ground.

How lucky he was that he'd thought of swiping a flashlight. The station was a shade of black so pure it would've put the darkness of the sky overhead to shame.

Standing on the edge of the platform, Alan clicked on the flashlight and tossed its beam into whatever crevice it would fit into. It wasn't as though he *expected* someone else to be here, but it'd been a while since he'd last paid this place a visit, so he thought he should just make sure.

It seemed empty enough. He set the flashlight down facing the opposite platform, stepped onto the tracks, picked up the flashlight, and climbed back up on the other side.

The restrooms were like two voids. Or a pair of pure, solid black eyes, watching him with not a sliver of emotion. It was unsettling. He decided to let whatever was in that darkness *remain* in the darkness, and so the beam of his flashlight never ventured beyond either of those doors.

Alan made for the usual payphone. He threw open the door, dialed in the number, and—

A deviation from the usual script, there was no waiting today. Hardly half a second from when the final number was dialed, the call was answered.

Alan had meant to apologize for not turning up. He had been rehearsing his lines all through his walk here, but the suddenness of the answer sent all of it crashing out of his mind.

"U-Um, yes, good evening," he stammered.

"That what they call this time of day where you're from?"

No growling? Alan thought, taken aback. Well, he seemed to be in a good mood, so now was as good a time to apologize as any.

"Hey, listen," Alan said seriously. "About today, I just wanted to—"

A snort on the end of the line cut him off.

"Forget it," said the murderer.

"What?" Alan said, a little more sharpness to it than he'd meant.

"I said forget it, it's fine."

What on earth was happening? In Alan's mind, convicted murderers were not exactly the epitome of compassion and forgiveness.

It shocked Alan, certainly. But what the murderer said next did not just shock him. It blew the wind right out of him and sent every nerve in his body tingling with fear.

"The cops, they stopped by, didn't they?"

A bead of sweat appeared on Alan's brow. "How do you know that?"

The murderer laughed as though Alan's confusion amused him. "Believe me, I know a lot more than that. For instance, it wasn't *really* the cops who held you back was it?" There was a pause. More than anything, Alan wished for it to stay. He had a sinking feeling that he knew what was coming, but when it actually came, it still sent him slumping against the cold glass wall. "No, it wasn't the cops. It was your wife, wasn't it?"

"Where are you?" Alan said, not bothering to keep the fear out of his voice. "How do you know all this? Who are you?"

"No one ever taught you not to ask more than one question at a time?" There was a short pause, marred by the sound of Alan's harsh breaths. "Where am I? I'm somewhere, I can tell you. I've got to be *somewhere*, right? Well, it depends." *What the hell is this guy on about?* Alan thought.

"Anyway, I can't tell you my exact location, obviously, but I can tell you this: I'm close. Much, much closer than you could ever imagine."

Alan shivered. Resisting the urge to turn around, he said, "Close to what? My current location, my house, what?"

"It depends. I told you already, didn't I?"

"It depends on *what*, exactly?"

There was a pause. A *long* pause.

"If you were attentive, you would've noticed that your first two questions were very closely related. You could reasonably extrapolate one from the other." The man's voice dropped a notch, so Alan had to strain his ears to hear him. "Problem is, I don't think you'll like *either* answer."

"Why? You've already told me that you're close, so what difference does it make if I know *how* close?"

"You won't like it. You think you can take the truth, but believe me, you can't. My advice? Don't poke the bear a second time. You've poked it once, had it wake up, stare you dead in the eyes, and decide to leave you alone. Second time, that bear's gonna maul you." The man chuckled, perhaps amused by his own analogy. "The third question you asked... What was it, again?"

"I asked who you are."

"Ah, yes, yes. Who I am. I'm just someone. I'm sure you know well enough that I'm not too interested in letting you know my identity."

Alan felt his heart thumping in his chest. "A-Anyway, let's get back to what we scheduled this whole thing for in the first place. Are there any particular kills that you'd like to talk about? Maybe the victim was unique in some way, or the reason you did it was something unconventional."

Alan was rambling, of course, but who could blame him? As far as he was concerned, a murderer had been watching him and his wife through a window for an entire day. Otherwise it made no sense for him to know the things that he did.

"No, I'm not in the mood today," the murderer said, much to Alan's surprise; he usually talked about his kills the way a parent would talk about their favorite child. "It's late right now. This is a cowardly time to be talking about crime. If you're gonna do it, do it in broad daylight."

Alan couldn't help but smile. Yes, that sounded a lot more like him. Rash, unreasonable, but, despite the quarter of a century of scalps beneath his bed, oddly endearing.

"What's say, oh, I don't know, next Thursday. Whatever date that is. And, I'll do you a solid. You seem to like these cowardly times when no one will catch you, so, just this once, we can have our talk at this time."

"I'll have to check my schedule, but for now let's say it's fine."

"Your schedule, ay?" the man said with a chuckle. "Yeah, go give it a peek. Be sure to get back to me if it happens to be filled up. I'm *sure* we can find a day that works."

Alan did not like his tone. It was supercilious. Condescending. As though he didn't think there was as much to Alan's schedule as he was making out—which, mind you, was completely true. But it was the murderer's *assumption* of it being true that ticked him off.

It was several seconds before his mind left behind his internal rant and returned to the conversation at hand.

Alan was startled—there was no one on the line. He had not realized when the silence had taken form. Well, the man had said he would be busy for a while. But, still, to just hang up with no notice whatsoever? Murderer or not, it annoyed him.

Alan remained listening with predatory acuity, attempting to pick up on any noise at all streaming through.

But there was none. The line was as silent as a graveyard. And so Alan did the only thing he could think of in that moment: He hung up. For a second he had a sinking feeling that he'd regret that, but then he gave it a second thought: What was the use of staying on the line when the man on the other end had long since left?

And so, Alan Michaels, a flashlight in one hand and a blank look on his face, turned to look at the moon. It appeared a little darker than usual through the glass of the payphone booth. Alan stared at the pale, cratered orb, now round and proud and full, but oblivious to the fact that the sun would shortly come and hide it away, hide it behind its massive, glorious light, until the evening came.

Alan sighed, feeling small all of a sudden.

Chapter 11

Alan Michaels would never have admitted it, but there was one fear in particular he had acquired in his childhood, and to this day it had never left him.

The dark. It terrified Alan to an unhealthy degree. It wasn't as people tended to say, that people were scared of what's *in* the dark, rather than the darkness *itself*. No, with Alan, he *was* scared of the dark, and not any imaginary monsters that may have found refuge in it. At some point, he'd concluded that it had to do with the fog—there were things in the dark, but he simply could not perceive them. That incompleteness, that in-the-darkness, if you will, was what Alan hated.

But today, the script was flipped. Alan stood in the dark of the payphone's booth, the flashlight dangling loosely from his fingers, painting the ground at his feet a color that could only be considered eerie, and he stood without a single fear in his mind.

However, that may have been more due to the fact that each and every one of his mental faculties were occupied at the moment.

He had never thought about it prior to this very moment, but now he simply had to: *who is this man?* Alan had simply been filing away his interactions with this man as something remote, in a sense; this man—this *convict*—was from an entirely different universe from Alan, a universe he believed could only ever be reached via this payphone. Two universes that Alan wholeheartedly never expected would collide.

So, then, what was all this? How could a person from a different universe to his own be privy to things happening in his?

The cops came over, didn't they?

It wasn't the cops who held you back, was it? No, it was your wife.

In a state of unawareness toward his actions, Alan punched the wall of the booth, sending a dull thud echoing inside the glass cage.

"How the hell do you know all this?"

There Alan stood, his punching hand numb but remaining on the glass.

He couldn't take this. He had to find a way to figure out who this man was...

But then what?

He was a convicted murderer. He held no hesitation, no remorse at all towards the act of murder, never mind the mere act of inflicting harm. If Alan were stupid enough to confront him, he'd be lucky to only end up in the hospital.

Ideas flocked to him. The problem was, they came often—too often. So often that, rather comically, he didn't have time to read his own thoughts; he'd be decrypting one thought, but before he'd get very far, another would come along and block it out. Try to decrypt that, another overlaps.

For lack of a better way to put it, his head was in a resounding mess.

Alan stood and thought, and thought, and thought...

Then, all of a sudden, he blinked: The flashlight had flickered.

Well, that was a problem. Some of his wits still about him, Alan decided to leave; being forced to navigate through the dark of the station? Not an attractive prospect.

He looked up from the ground—and was startled to see something red. No, not quite red, actually, but more like scarlet. He eyed this very same scarlet, resting upon on one of the buttons of the payphone, a little startled. He tried wiping it away with his thumb, but to no avail. Alan stared. The amber wasn't only on *that* button, he now realized. It was on *every* button, and always in the same spot, the bottom right.

Wait... I've turned the flashlight off, so how can I still see?

Another moment of thought was all it took, and Alan understood what was happening, and he wheeled around. His arms shot up, shielding his eyes.

The sun was creeping over the horizon, slow and silent as a lizard about to attack a fly.

Alan was shocked. Had he really been standing motionless for so long that the sunrise had come? Evidently, that was the case.

His shock never vanished. For a moment it had merely detoured toward the sudden brightness and his whiling away the morning unnoticed, but in an instant it was back where it belonged. Back on the murderer's words.

Alan shook his head, remembering that he was supposed to be home before Nala woke. That *had* been the plan, but that was before the murderer had thrown this spectacular screw into the works. Forget going home, Alan needed to bring some sense of control—some normalcy—back into his life. That was all he could think of to take his mind off of this debacle.

And so Alan pushed open the door, passed by the restrooms, which now seemed a lot more like they were just two doors designed to allow entry rather than a pair of eyes.

Alan decided to leave the flashlight in a tall patch of grass right by the platform; who knows, maybe it'd come in handy in the future. He then crossed over to the other platform, walked out the gaping doorway a little ways off, and there he was, back in the outside world. The *normal* world.

Alan began to walk. His destination? Chloe's Café. A toast and a coffee, and maybe eavesdropping on a couple dementia-fueled stories. That was just what he needed to set his day back on track—if it *could* be set back on track, which a large part of him doubted.

But still, he had to try. If the murderer could watch him, then Alan needed to prove that he was not afraid.

"Hello, delicatessen," he said aloud.

Some would perhaps consider this interaction a sign of brewing insanity, but not Alan. He was terribly eager for a touch of familiarity, and that big conglomeration of brick and glass on the corner was the only thing here that he was at all familiar with.

The walk did not feel longer, but it certainly felt heavier, like there was an anchor in his heart.

He shook his head again, trying to clear his thoughts. *No point thinking about weird stuff.*

Soon he was back in the parts of town where other humans were not merely an urban legend. And what that meant was that, soon enough he'd arrive back in their own little corner of town. And what did *that* mean? It meant, quite simply, that bacon and toast were close.

But then, along the way, something unexpected stole his attention. Alan stopped walking, dumbstruck, and began to stare.

On the other side of the street, two young people were walking. Brother and sister, probably. They were headed in the opposite direction to Alan, and they were still quite some way off. They seemed to be in their early twenties. They were chatting away, both seeming excited about something.

Neither of them took any notice of Alan. That was unsurprising, but what *was* surprising was the fact that *he* had taken notice of *them*. He could not fathom why he'd take such close notice of two random people in the street. It had never happened before. Even prior to getting married, the only woman he'd ever taken notice of was Nala. Although, in Alan's defense, his interest toward them was not at all similar to what he held towards his wife. It was... different. He could not place the feeling, and that made him a little antsy.

Well, then, who were these two? These two who managed to steal away the attention of a man who just wanted some toast?

Walking along the other side of the street, the two passed him by, still taking no notice of him. Unsure why, Alan breathed a sigh of relief.

He wished for nothing more than to just get on with his walk, but his feet refused to budge. In the end, rather shamefully, he craned his head around to watch the pair.

Something Alan hadn't counted on happened, causing his heart to miss a beat: The younger of the pair, perhaps feeling his unrelenting gaze on her, turned around. She looked him dead in the eyes, and his heart skipped another beat.

I know you, he thought, an odd feeling of elation welling up inside him. Then he doubled back. Of course he didn't know her. It was ridiculous... right?

The woman stopped walking and narrowed her eyes at him. Oh no. He knew what this was. He looked like one hell of a creep right about now, didn't he.

But then, contrary to any reaction Alan may have expected, the woman's eyes widened.

Alan was certain they were brother and sister now, and for the life of him he couldn't have explained it. It wasn't even as though they looked similar enough for most people's minds to arrive at that conclusion unprompted. No, he just *knew*.

The woman truly fit the bill of a youngest child: She was reckless and impulsive, and, judging by the look of unadulterated panic on her big brother's face, a constant cause of at least mild stress for her loved ones.

Without checking for traffic (of which there was a lot), she began to run across the street, making a beeline toward him. This stunt was met with quite a bit of sudden braking, a choir of horns blaring at a common enemy, and a hefty amount of surely-present swearing behind tinted windows.

Alan felt an instinct, almost a paternal instinct, to jump in and get her out of there. But it was not necessary, for the woman managed to arrive on his side not only unscathed, but in fact beaming, wholly oblivious to the havoc she had caused not five feet back.

Without so much as a word, the girl—no longer a woman in his eyes, but a girl—lunged forward and threw both her arms around him. Alan eyed the top of her head in confusion, his hands doing an odd dance over her head, unsure of what exactly they were meant to be doing.

Alan turned back to look across the street. Drivers and pedestrians gave him odd looks as they passed, but he didn't notice any of them. All he saw was the older one, his mouth agape. He suddenly felt as though he recognized him, too, but was again unsure as to how that could be true. The brother seemed just as surprised as he was by the girl's actions, but made no move to come and collect her.

The girl hugging him looked up, causing him to jerk his head toward her. The two stared at each other for a long, long time. Her eyes were bright and smiling, creases forming around the edges. His eyes were just plain confused.

"You don't remember me, do you?" the girl said, a teasing lilt to her voice.

"Um... No, I don't." He looked away, a little embarrassed, then met her eyes again. "Sorry."

"No, it's alright. It's happened before, after all. You've been that way ever since that accident." She nodded toward her brother, still rooted to the spot.

It took Alan a terribly long time to process what she'd just said.

"Wait... Wait," he said, his heart rate all of a sudden skyrocketing.

But the girl did not wait. She turned back toward him, and what she said next knocked any remaining wind right out of him.

"Anyway, hello, Dad. It's been a while, hasn't it?"

Chapter 12

"I thought you looked familiar!" Alan chuckled, his voice an odd mix of embarrassment and sarcasm.

"I could tell, Dad. Imagine our shock, we stumble into town on horseback 'cause we're too lazy to use our feet, and the first person we see? Our own dad." She buried her face in his chest, and, despite how bubbly her voice was, Alan could feel two wet spots forming on his shirt. Her hug got just a touch tighter. "God, I missed you, Dad."

Alan placed a gentle hand on the top of her head. With his other hand he scratched the back of his own head, not at all sure how to react to this. In the end, he decided to break the silence, and the way he did it could only be called wrongheaded.

"Well... Did you *actually* ride in on horseback?"

The girl—no, Madison. *Madison* laughed, and it was an entirely startled laugh, as though she couldn't quite believe that *this* was the first question she was being asked during such a precious moment.

"No, Dad, of course not." She peeled away from him with some reluctance. Her smile was still present, but her eyes glistened with wetness under the sunlight. She dabbed at her eyes with her sleeve. "It's a figure of speech. Me and Asher use it for when we get a cab even though we could easily just walk. It just means we treat ourselves well."

"Oh?" Alan said, ruffling her hair into a noodley mess. "What clever children I have. So young and already coming up with nonsensical uses of our language."

She chuckled. "It's in our blood, obviously."

She glanced at her brother, only now crossing the street to join them. He was not half as hectic as the younger had been, but it was clear he was trying hard to keep his feet from breaking away. The oldest was looking between Alan and Madison as he crossed.

"Hello, Asher," Alan said the moment he had reached them. "How are you? Everything's alright with you, I hope."

His little sister was busy occupying his chest, so Asher was forced to hug him around the back.

But before he did, he did something a little odd: He leaned forward and looked at his face.

"Dad," he said, a quiver to his voice. "Do you really remember us?"

"Yes, Asher. Of course I remember you two."

He had forgotten them. As pretty as the words Alan painted were, the truth of the matter was that, right up until a minute or two ago, the fact that he'd had kids at all had escaped him.

"Sorry, kids. It's been a while. You've both grown, so it took me a little bit to recognize you." Alan looked to the side out of guilt. He couldn't believe he was making an excuse for not remembering his own children. "That accident, you know? It messed me up. It messed me up *bad*. The other guy was killed on the spot, so I'm lucky to have gotten off with just a couple of scars and some difficulty tapping into my memories, you know?"

Both of them flinched, causing Alan to startle rather badly himself. He was sure they'd meant for it to be furtive, but he caught them sharing an odd look.

"Yeah. We remember the accident. Mom was absolutely frantic, thinking something happened to you," Asher said. "And it's not your fault for not recognizing us. It's impressive you still know our faces after all this time."

"Well..." Alan said, feeling a little shy from all the compliments. "It *has* been a while, hasn't it?"

"It has, Dad," Madison said. "It really has. But, never mind that for now. We're starving over here. We got held up in traffic for an hour, maybe more."

"What?" Alan said, surprised. "Why didn't you guys have breakfast? Actually, forget that. What time is it now, and when did you leave?"

"Whoa, whoa, calm it, Dad. One at a time," Madison said. "First, we didn't have breakfast since we didn't think we'd be held up that long. We wanted to leave our appetites intact for home cooking. Second," she said, shaking back her sleeve and eyeing her watch, "it's a little past eight-thirty. And third, we left at, oh, I don't know, six?" She turned to Asher for confirmation, but all the input Asher had to offer was a shrug. Madison clicked her tongue. "Yeah, six, I think."

"The cabbie was alright? No problems, right? Nothing weird happened to you?"

"We took three separate cabs today, an old man, a young man, and a very quiet man whose age I can't guess. All of them were perfectly good people."

"Well, that's good."

Now he ruffled Asher's hair. He seemed a bit more annoyed by it than his sister had been.

"I was just going down to the diner for some breakfast. Would you guys like to join me?"

The pair glanced at each other, then beamed back at him. "Would we!" Madison said. "Now, let's get going, Dad, before my stomach starts eating itself."

The usual tinkle came to signal his entry. The usual smells of savory and sweet wafted in the air. And the usual crowd of about five people were offering their patronage.

Everything was as it tended to be, so why did Alan feel so out of place? Was it because he had his children with him? No, no one here was paying either him or them any mind. It couldn't have been that. Maybe his talk with the murderer was the root of this feeling. But, then again, that was a feeling entirely separate from this, and that had been bothering him ever since the talk. *This* feeling, however, was brand new, having sprung up the moment the front doors of Chloe's Café had come open in welcome of him.

"Dad?"

"Huh?" he said, looking up sharply.

Asher and Madison were staring at him, their eyes drowned mostly in worry, but also something else, something he could not quite put his finger on.

"Are you alright? You looked a little pale right then. You're not sick, are you?" Asher asked, sounding more like his father than his child.

"Yes, yes, I'm fine," he said, not at all feeling the truth in those words. "I just remembered something I was supposed to have mailed yesterday. It's alright, though."

Madison seemed to have accepted that without any arguments, but Asher, perhaps due to his status as the eldest, was a little more shrewd.

"They accept mail on Christmas day? Since when?"

Damn.

"No, they don't," he said to stall for time. Within a half second he came up with what he believed to be as clever of an excuse as he was going to cook up. "I meant mail as in to drop in the mail box, not to hand over to the post office."

"Oh," Asher said.

He was silent for a moment, causing Alan to worry about whether he'd pursue it further. But he shrugged, and that was that.

Alan led his children to his usual booth, and a moment later Chloe came scuttling up. She cocked her head, seeming mildly surprised to see these two unusual guests.

"Who are these two?" she asked Alan, genuine curiosity in her voice.

He smiled playfully, then told Chloe, "Take a good, hard look at them."

She squinted at them, and she stared, and stared, and went on staring. Even the children, despite the promise of food dangling tantalizingly close to their hungry noses, seemed amused by the interaction.

"Nope," Chloe said at last. "No idea."

"Really?" he said. He pointed at his face, then at the two of them. "You don't see how my own children resemble me?"

Chloe's eyebrows raised in mild surprise. "You have kids?" she asked. "I've known you for, what, a year or so now? How has this never come up?"

"They've been away from home, see. I didn't want to talk about them, in case it made me miss them even more." A lie, of course, but one that was both workable *and* endearing.

"Aww, how *adorable*," Chloe crooned. She turned toward Asher and Madison. "Such a good dad you two have. You'd better take care of him now, hear?"

"We were planning to," Asher said with a smile. He was sure everyone else took it at face value, but Alan detected the note of a challenge in his voice. He sighed, remembering. He'd always been like this, ever since he was little.

"Anyway, Chloe..."

Orders were given, fires were put on, stomachs rumbled, a young pair grumbled, and some ten minutes later Chloe returned with their food, two plates in her hands, one balanced masterfully on her forearm.

Alan had things he wanted to know, but it could wait. He left his own food untouched, instead opting to watch the two of them, their faces both split in wide grins as they threw back their breakfast. It was by no means a small meal, but they did a fantastic job at making it seem like just that.

Halfway through her meal, Madison suddenly stopped. Seeming to go a little pale, she began looking all around the table, as though she felt that something was out of place.

"No..." Madison trailed off, her voice sounding a little desperate.

Alan cocked his head. "What is it, Madison?" he said. "Is something wrong? Did Chloe forget something?"

"Ah. No, no, it's nothing," she said, but her eyes refused to meet his.

"So," Alan said as soon as two pairs of silverware were set on empty plates. "It's been a while. So, kids, tell me. How's life? What have you two been up to? How have things been going for you?

Madison giggled, and Asher rolled his eyes. "Dad, what is this, an interview? Relax a little. We're you're kids, you know."

"Yes, yes, I know. You guys know me. That's just the way I talk, even with your mother."

"Even with Mom, you speak like you're on a first date?"

"Yup. Always." He paused, took a sip of his coffee, then cleared his throat. "Anyway, what are you two doing with your lives? College? Internships?"

"Dad, you know we're in college. Both of us," Madison said. "I major in business, Asher majors in literature."

Alan raised his eyebrows. "Business? Since when were you interested in business?"

Madison cocked her head. "Dad, I've *always* been into business. Remember, I used to run a lemonade stand on the weekends when I was younger. Then there was this one time, I found that baseball card on the ground, so I dusted it off, and by the end of the week I'd managed to domino trade it into an encyclopedia."

"Really?" Alan said in awe. "That's incredible."

Madison peered into his eyes, her expression seeming a little hurt. "You mean you don't remember, dad?"

Alan looked into that pitiful little face. He couldn't take this feeling of inadequacy.

"No, I don't remember," he said, not willing to lie to his own children. He slumped forward so his forehead touched the edge of the table, then laced his fingers behind his head.

He hated this. His children, his own flesh and blood, and he knew not a damn thing about them. And it was all that damn accident's fault. For the first time since it had happened, he didn't think, *How lucky I am that I'm alive!* Nor did he think, *The other guy got off worst, so I shouldn't complain.*

No, in that moment, all he could think of was one thing: *If that damn idiot hadn't been speeding in the wrong direction, I wouldn't be going through all this.*

Was that what happened?

A small hand set itself gently upon his back. Alan looked up; Asher and Madison had both been sitting opposite him, but now the other side of the table was empty. The one who had her hand on his back was Madison. She had squeezed in next to him, and Asher was standing beside her, a look that was a mixture of concern and pity welling up in his eyes.

"It's alright, Dad, it's alright," Madison whispered, her tone mellow. "It's not your fault. It's the accident. It really screwed you up, didn't it?"

Alan nodded, and the three of them remained that way for a short while.

"Feel better now?" Asher asked.

"Yeah, I do," Alan said. It was not a lie; something deep inside of him truly seemed to have been soothed by the simple act.

"Well, Dad, let's forget about us for a second. Tell us what *you've* been up to recently. Are you still writing?" Asher asked. "You're the reason I got interested in literature to begin with. If you're not writing anymore, I'll feel just a *little* hard done by, for sure."

Alan laughed. "Don't worry. I'm still writing. Well... Attempting to, at least."

"What do you mean *attempting* to?"

"Well, I've had some ideas. One or two fantastic ones, some alright, but most of the lot mediocre. I've gotten as far as the research. But that's it. I've been *trying* to write, don't get me wrong. I've been sitting at this exact spot every day for, what, two months now? Words just refuse to get onto the paper.

"What, writer's block?"

"Sort of, but not quite." Alan paused and gazed out of the window. "It's more like, I've got the blueprints, I've got the material and the manpower, everyone knows what to do, everyone's *ready* to do what they are supposed to... And yet, no work ever gets done. I've got everything I had when I was world-class, but it's like my pencil and paper are repelling each other."

"Mmm," said Asher with a nod. As someone from the literary world himself, Alan was certain he knew what he was talking about.

"But why all of a sudden?" Madison asked.

Alan sighed. "All of it comes back to the accident, really. See, Madison, you might remember that before the accident, I was always so—"

"Ow!" Madison yelped. She turned to her brother and gave him the stink eye. "The heck is your problem, Ash? I'm trying to have a civilized—ow!"

Alan had no clue at all what was happening, but he laughed. Madison was not amused by her brother's antics.

"For God's sake, Ash! Stop! Are you a crab? Why are you pinching me all of a sudd—ow ow ow!"

"You two finished?" Alan asked, not at all attempting to keep the amusement out of his voice. He turned to look at Asher. "What was that about, Asher?"

"Don't worry about it, dad."

Alan shrugged. "If you say so." He turned to Madison. "Anyway, as I was saying, prior to the accident, I was—"

He was cut off again, this time by the sharp ring of falling cutlery.

"Sorry, sorry," Madison said, ducking beneath the table to collect it.

Alan eyed her through the table as though he had X-ray vision, his eyes narrowed in confusion. "Madison, did you just..."

She peeked over the table. "Did I what, Dad?" she asked, her voice innocent.

Alan eyed her for a moment, shook his head, then muttered, "No, never mind. It was just my imagination."

Fallen? No, no. *Dropped.* Yes, she had dropped them. He had seen her rather sad attempt at sleight of hand as she picked them up. It was no accident; it was her intention to cut him off.

"Alright, then, Dad. Let's get going. Mom'll be feeling lonely right about now."

"Ah. Yes, yes, let's get going," he said, entirely forgetting about his own breakfast, sitting untouched and still warm upon the table.

Asher paid, and the three of them set out of the front door together. Their pace was the same, and their gaits were the same, but an obvious air of awkwardness had settled between them.

Alan did not notice it. He was too busy thinking.

He had been cut off twice. *Intentionally* cut off twice. Both times, he had been about to bring up his life prior to the accident—prior to all his memories being either rearranged or lost.

It didn't take long for Alan to reach the most logical conclusion: There was something about his past that his kids wished to *leave* in the past. An aspect of himself that had been lost in the accident, and one they were glad he had lost.

Alan stroked his chin as he cast a furtive look at each of his children. He smiled.

Like it or not, kids, you can't keep your mouths shut forever.

Chapter 13

Thursday morning. This time he did not forget, for he had written it down. Just in case anyone went through his notes, he was clever enough not to put down something like: *coming Thursday - chat with convicted murderer*. Instead what he put was this: *2T* (meaning the second day of the week that began with a 'T') - KM (not kilometer. The K was for Killer, and, on the very decentchance that his future self was too dense to understand that much, the M was for Murderer).

Sneaking out was no longer an option. At least, not a workable one. He had *three* people he would have to get past now, and two of them slept lightly enough to have woken to a pin drop.

Since it was no longer an option, Alan decided to do the exact *opposite* of sneaking out; he would do what he needed to do as though it were already late into the morning.

Instead of tiptoeing around in utter silence as though he were conducting a robbery, Alan got out of bed as he normally would, washed up in the bathroom—making no attempt to conceal the noise of the water as he did so—grabbed his coat from off its hook, and stepped outside of the room.

He went upstairs to where Asher and Madison were sleeping, turned on the hallway light, planted a couple of light knocks on their door, then twisted the doorknob. He opened the door the tiniest bit, sending a wedge of light leaking into the room. He peered in at the tiny gap of the door—and he chuckled.

Such light sleepers, my babies.

They were staring at him, their eyes squinted in the annoyed, tired way that seemed to be exclusive to people who had just been woken up from a pleasant sleep.

Alan opened the door a little wider and stepped inside. "Hello, kids."

"Hello, Dad," Madison said. "What are you doing up at a time like this? Also, would you mind shutting the door? The hallway light's hurting my eyes."

"Oh, yeah, sorry."

He swung the door shut with a dull thud.

"Anyway, kids, I won't be here long, so just listen for a second, alright?"

"Mhmm. What is it, Dad?" It was Asher this time. He had his head back on his pillow, clearly uninterested in what he had to say.

"I'm going out for a little bit."

They both shot up in bed, and the dark did nothing to hide the fact that their eyes had widened in fear.

Alan took a startled step back, kicking the door by accident. "What sort of reaction is that, you two? What's gotten into you?"

"You're going out where exactly, Dad, at this time?" Madison asked.

"I'm just stopping by the..." He had been about to say the park, but something stopped him, and he diverted at the last second. "...parking lot. The parking lot." He saw the two share a strange look, so he went on, "It's empty and quiet over there. I thought it'd be good for my writing, maybe."

His children just stared at him, wordless. He did not understand why they had such a strong reaction toward this. Did they think he couldn't take care of himself?

Alan waited another moment in case they had anything to say. They didn't, so he filled the silence on his own.

"Anyway, kids, I came to ask you to do me a favor. If your Mom comes and asks where I am, I want you to tell her just what I told you."

The pair remained silent for a long, long time. It was Madison who found her voice first. "Will you be long, Dad?"

"A few hours, maybe longer. Depends how my writing's going, I guess."

"Well, alright, then." She observed him closely. *Very* closely. "You stay out of trouble, hear?"

"Of course." He opened the door and stepped outside. And then he shut the door, leaving his two children in the pleasant dark of the early morning.

Alan had taken the liberty to oil the front door the day after his previous talk, and so there was no need for him to demonstrate his remarkable dexterity by climbing his way out through the window for a second time.

Alan had his satchel with him this time. Inside were a couple of pens, a dozen or so pencils, a sharpener, an eraser, and—an addition he had made just for this trip—a little notepad. This time, he would be taking notes as the murderer talked.

And, the thing he was most proud of: his book—no longer blank!

Yes, after all that procrastinating, Alan had finally managed to pen something down. In fact, more impressive than that, he had managed to catch up to *all* the murderer's stories so far. All of that was enough to fill a hundred and fifty pages, more or less.

The walk went as it usually did: long, dark, silent, but without hiccups. Alan arrived at the station and did his usual dismounting and remounting onto the opposite platform.

As Alan made his way to the farthest payphone, he flipped open his satchel. From inside he produced the notepad and both pens—couldn't risk one running dry, now, could he?

He stepped inside the booth, and before the door had even swung shut behind him, his free hand had picked up the phone and was dialing in the number.

The cowardly hours, Alan thought to himself, looking around, taking in everything the world had to offer. *Yes, I like the sound of that. It's got a nice ring to it.*

This time would be different, Alan could tell. The lump of nervous excitement in his stomach agreed. It had never been there before.

Alan waited for the murderer to appear on the line. With each passing second his nerves sang a shriller tune, and when it reached its crescendo, Alan felt close to exploding. And then, finally:

Click.

"You're here earlierthan I expected," the murderer said. "Thought you'd get held up looking for a way to sneak past that wife of yours."

"No need to worry about that. I've dealt with it, so I didn't have to do any sneaking today."

"Oh, you've dealt with it, have you?" the man said, amused. "I'm curious as to what you mean by that. But we can leave it aside for now. This whole arrangement is for *you* to interview *me*, isn't it?"

"Yes, it is. So, as I asked the last time, are there any particular kills you're proud of?"

"I'm proud of every kill I get away with, aesthetics and processes be damned. But if you want me to talk, we should pick up from last time, shouldn't we?" Alan could hear the devilish grin in the man's voice as he spoke. "One or two. Show me."

Alan thought about it for a moment, then did exactly what he had done the last time: Hand concealed behind his back, he held up a peace sign. That same instant, the murderer clicked his tongue.

"Two again, huh?" he growled. "You're one lucky bastard, I'll tell you what. One was the bad one this time around."

Perhaps idiotically, that made Alan feel just a little regretful. He found himself wishing he had picked the other option, just for the sake of satisfying his curiosity, if nothing else. He jotted the fact of the feeling down in his notes. It had been just over a week, but he had completely forgotten about the flashlight in the grass, instead opting to write in the dark and hoping it would later be legible.

"So, two, huh?" the man said.

He sank into what seemed to be thoughtful silence for a moderately long moment. When his voice reappeared on the line, it was as though he had taken a hit of something energizing.

"Two. Quite the specimen, that woman was." He sounded bubbly almost to the point of insanity, as though he were a child who had just found someone else who liked his obscure hobby. "She *was* a specimen before I'd met her, of course. After that? Not so much."

"Well, what was the reason you did it? And how did you do it?"

"One at a time, I told you. The reason? See, that's a little complicated. You're a writer, so maybe you would understand if I put it like this." There was a pause, and if Alan had been on a seat, he would've found himself on the edge of it. "Sometimes when you write, it's not as if every single scene is planned, is it? Sometimes you just go, 'Hey, this seems like it could work,' and you throw it in. There's no real *reason* to that, just a well-chiseled intuition. This is the same. If you're looking for a specific reason, I ain't got one. Something visceral inside of me wanted it done, so I did it."

"Mmm," Alan said, still jotting all this down. He hated to admit it, but he found all of this rather interesting. "So, how did this kill go exactly? Did it happen at the victim's home, or did you take it somewhere else?"

"I don't kill at people's homes. That's as stupid as stupid gets. I plant stuff like hair or sweat or blood occasionally, but that's all I do as far as their homes are concerned."

For some reason, the man laughed.

"How did I do it, you wonder? Keep your pen close to your pad, kid, 'cause you'll be needing it." Alan did as he was told. "Now, you know how people tend to have a pair of most things? Eyes, ears, feet, whatever."

"Mhmm, yes," Alan said, trying hard to remain calm. He felt a cold lump in his stomach, for he was sure he knew where this was going.

"Well, once I was done with her, this woman was missing some of her parts that were meant to come in pairs. The right foot, the right hand, the right eye. I removed them, but not in that order. No, you always want to start with the hands. Gives 'em less of a chance at fighting back. Believe me, most people, injured or not, will fight back. But in this case, the order wouldn't have mattered much. The woman was a princess at home, probably never taken a rubber band flick, never burned herself on a frying pan. Take someone like that and saw their hand off at the wrist? The pain completely paralyzed her, and you'd best believe that made my life a whole lot easier. Didn't pop a squeak when I did the same to her foot, or when I wrenched her eye out like I was removing the yolk from a hard-boiled egg—God, I love symmetry. Anyway, she just lay there, breathing hard. Killing people like that can be boring, let me tell you. They just sit there and take their fate, no arguments, no pleading, nothing."

Alan found that he had stopped taking notes. He was only listening now, dumbstruck, thinking to himself: *How gruesome. How disgusting... How... How...*

How beautiful.

Alan recoiled as though he had just been shot. How on earth did that thought creep its way into his brain?

Alan shook his head and rubbed at his face. "Okay, I've gotten all that down." He paused for a moment, allowing his thoughts to rearrange themselves. "So, where did this happen?"

There was a pause. Alan drummed his fingers on the side of the payphone, and by the time he had counted to a hundred, there was still no answer.

"Hello?" Alan said a little louder. No reply.

"Hello!" Alan said, now yelling into the receiver. The man had gone. "What about our next talk? When will it be?"

There was no answer. Of course there wasn't; the murderer had already hung up.

Alan hung up as well, annoyed. This was the second time he's done this. Such a blatant lack of respect.

But, what could good guy Alan do about it? He could heave a heavy-hearted sigh and gaze up at the pitch-black sky, that's what.

Alan was not much in the mood to even pretend to attempt to write today. He walked his couple of miles home, threw his satchel on the nightstand, plopped himself in bed, and, despite the clock not having struck ten a.m. yet, it was off to dreamland for Alan.

It was a fantastic sleep, dreamless and uninterrupted. As far as Alan knew, he hadn't even rolled over a single time. And yet, when he awoke nearly a full day later, he was sure that could not have been the case, for his hands were covered in black patches. Soot? Dust? Alan had no clue, nor did he care. He went to the bathroom, washed it off, and that was that.

Several days passed, and Alan once more found himself whiling the morning away at Chloe's Café. He was twirling his pencil, but he had no real intention of writing.

There was a tinkle, and Alan whipped his head toward the entrance to see who it was—false alarm, just a customer.

Alan may have forgotten most things if he didn't write them down, but he did not for a second forget his theory. He needed to confirm it, and now he was waiting for that tinkle, followed by that exclamation. An exclamation that just two months ago had been indiscernible from the bark of a dog or the purr of a cat to Alan.

He twirled his pencil with one hand, drumming on the table with the fingers of the other. He was growing more and more impatient with every tinkle that turned out to be someone else. A little more, just a little more, and his patience would be rewarded...

And then, quite suddenly, it arrived.

Tinkle.

"Papers!"

Alanwas standing in front of the man before the words had entirely left his mouth. Alan didn't have small change, so he stuffed a whole dollar into the man's bag, and within half a second he was back in his seat.

Yesterday, the paper had been clean. As Alan flipped the pages, he begged for that not to be the case today as well. There was only so much suspense his heart could take.

Flip. Flip. Flip.

There has to be something by now, surely. There has to be. There just has to be...

Flip. Flip. Flip. Flip. Fli—hold on, what was that?

Alan turned back a page, and in the bottom right corner, printed in the tiniest print the press must've had, was just what Alan had been looking for.

There had been a murder. There was a picture of the corpse. Alan felt his heart lunge out of his throat. It wasn't the gruesomeness that did it to him, but the familiarity.

This was not his first time seeing that image. It was his second.

The first time? Not two days ago, when Alan had brought to mind this very same image while someone was telling him a story.

The corpse was bloodied all over, its expression mangled as though it had died from pain rather than anything else. Yes, it was familiar, indeed, and with its missing right eye, stolen right hand and foot, Alan could almost hazard a guess as to who had done this.

Alan scanned the article for an estimate, and he found it near the end of the article:

Investigators believe the incident to have taken place at approximately 3:42 a.m. yesterday.

Alan chuckled to himself. His talk had happened several days ago.

Is this an astronomical coincidence as well, Michaels?

It was ugly, and it was dirty, and perhaps it made Alan himself, though inadvertently, a conspirator. But it was the truth.

Alan Michaels' murderous call mate was not telling him about *past* murders.

He was telling him about *future* ones.

Chapter 14

That night was one of the worst Alan had ever been through. Nala had long since fallen asleep—it said a lot about his mental state that he had forgotten to bid her good night. There's a first time for everything, they often say, but Alan suspected that wasn't quite meant for things like this.

Alan looked calm enough as he lay in bed. His chest rose and fell in an even rhythm, which was odd in itself, considering his heart had been hammering away inside his ribcage ever since he had left the diner.

But his demeanor told nothing of his true condition. Since the moment he'd stepped out of that diner, he'd been in something of a clueless stupor. The familiarity of home did nothing to cure him. All day he had been gazing up at the ceiling, and by now he had grown familiar enough with it to tell you the story of each individual flake of plaster.

"What a damned mess," he said, soft enough for only himself and nobody else to hear.

He had suspected it, of course. He had been close to perfectly certain of what was happening, ever since the moment he had seen the report about the pink-haired Alan, a mirror image of the murderer's words.

So did that mean he was an accomplice?

But, now that he knew that he had been right all along? Now it was different. Now he had a responsibility to do something. He was not speaking to a man who had turned over a new leaf, who had left his broken past behind and done all he could to get his life back on track. No, this man was a cold-blooded killer through and through.

Alan felt a great weight settle on his shoulders. He may well have been the only one who knew what was going on. He had to do something with this knowledge. He *had* to.

But what?

Should he let it marinate for a little, then go confront him, make him spill what exactly it was he was trying to achieve here?

Or should he pretend he didn't even know what a newspaper was and get as much content out of this man as he possibly could?

The human part of him, the part that had a wife and kids to watch over, favored the first option.

The writer's part of him, the part that wanted to create a page-turner of the sort that nobody had ever seen, told him to keep going. He was not going after Alan, so who cared?

But there was a third option. The most obvious option in all of this:

Why not just go to the police?

Yes, of course. He would just have to go to the police, the other two options be damned. Yes, just get out of bed, throw on his jacket, and head on to the police station. They would hear him out, and they would dispatch whoever it was they needed to dispatch. And they'd round the guy up, take him in, boom, problem solved.

Just go to the cops, it was so simple...

No.

Alan remembered what the murderer had said: *Sometimes, there's no real reason to it, just a well-chiseled intuition.*

Alan's own intuition, as well-chiseled as it was ever going to be, told him this:

Keep the cops out of this. You'll regret it otherwise.

Why? Why would he, a normal, law-abiding citizen regret reporting this to the cops?

No. He appreciated his instincts, for they tended to provide him with solutions before he'd even figured out the problem. But, today, his instincts were wrong. He would not let that murderer hurt another person from his community.

And so Alan remained gazing at the ceiling, now a little more relaxed. And he waited, waited for the pitch-black of the ceiling to turn just a touch lighter, signaling the coming of dawn.

The moment it came, Alan was off.

With all the conviction in the world, Alan did what he had to do: Right then and there, at whatever in the morning it was, he threw some water on his face to freshen himself up, threw on his sweater with quite some aggression, and headed out the front door, making for the police station.

It felt a little odd to him, heading out at this time, but not for the old payphones. Quite the opposite, in fact. If things went to plan, then he'd *never* have to return to those decrepit things. They could converse with whatever was in the restrooms for all he cared.

It was not hard to find the police station. For starters, it had squad cars of black and white filling up its tiny car park out back. Also, it was the only place in the civilized parts of town that would have its lights on at such an odd hour.

There were not two cops as there had been last time, but five. Two sat behind their computers, their faces dyed the color of the screens before them, and three on the front row of five-by-five waiting seats meant for visitors. Not the spindly chairs at the counter, but right behind those.

It was an odd feeling, Alan could tell you. Alan had been hearing laughing and playful slapping wedged into their conversation when he had been outside. But now, it was dead silent.

Alan was the second largest person in the room, behind only his pal from last time. But with ten eyes staring at him, ten eyes that, at the drop of a hat, at the slightest of movements they didn't like, could cuff him and throw him behind bars (perhaps in his stress of the situation, Alan did not realize that that was quite simply not allowed), he felt exceptionally small.

"Well, what'll it be this time, sir?" asked the man at the counter. "If you're here for a sequel of last time, I'm sorry to tell you that my answer hasn't changed. As members of law enforcement, we do our utmost to keep civilians *out* of trouble. We have no incentive to be throwing you into the fire just because that's where you want to be. Please, have a seat, by the way."

His standing by the door was intentional. He disliked the prospect of having to occupy one of those spindly chairs. There would be two cops facing him, three more behind him. He would feel trapped. Unsafe. Like a gazelle in a ring of lions. No, Alan did not like it one bit. From here he could watch all five of them at once. None of them could sneak up on him, none of them could—

"Sir?" said one of the cops in the front row. He stood up and made for Alan, causing him to flinch. The man noticed but did not relent. "Sir, I think it's best if you sit." He placed a gentle hand on Alan's shoulder and guided him into the seat. Then he turned and sat back on his seat. A front row seat to this oncoming train wreck.

"Sir, it's got nothing to do with last time, right? If so, like I said, we can't help you. If you're hell-bent on wanting to talk to the guy, you'll have to tap into the black market for his number or address." The man gave Alan a quick, probing look, as though gauging whether he found any of those ideas attractive. Alan's expression remained slack and unchanged, so the man went on, "I wouldn't recommend that, though. Risky business, the black market. We're forced to dive into it every now and again ourselves, usually to catch arms dealers, and even we don't like it."

"No, no," Alan said. "It's got nothing to do with last time. You told me it's a bad idea, so I decided to do away with it." The cop gave an approving nod, and Alan went on, "I'm here today to make a report."

Just like last time, this caveman of a cop picked up his pencil and a sheet of paper despite having a perfectly healthy computer right in front of him.

"What is it about?"

"You know how even yesterday there was a report about a murder in the news?"

The cop nodded. "About as brutal as they come, that."

"Yes," Alan said in agreement. "Well, see, the thing is, I—" He cut the rest of his sentence off. He did not subtly trail off, as though it were a gentle curve. It was more like someone had grabbed his throat as he was speaking, sending everything unsaid falling off a cliff.

"Yes, sir, what is it?" the cop said, straightening himself up to his full height. Even sitting, he seemed a terribly imposing presence.

"Sorry, give me a second." Alan stared at the top of the counter, his heart suddenly thundering. The cop wheeled his chair round, got a cup of water from the dispenser behind him, and set it down next to Alan. His attention not quite there, Alan picked it up and threw it back in a single draught.

"Better now?" The cop's voice held genuine concern. It made Alan smile.

Alan wiped his mouth with his sleeve. "Yes, much better. Thank you."

A short moment of respectful silence fell between them.

"Sir, that murder you mentioned—and I don't mean to stress you up by saying this—but we've got no clues as to who did it. You'd think if someone did something this gruesome, they would've left something, right?" The man closed his eyes, stuck out his bottom lip, and shook his head slowly. "Not a damn hair. Brutal and savage, but also calculated. The kind of person who knows what they're doing. And the kind *we* hate dealing with."

"You've got no clues at all?" Alan asked genuinely surprised.

"No, sir, not one. That's why, if you know something—anything—about this, then please tell us. Even if it's something seemingly irrelevant about the victim, like she was into sewing or something, just say it. The irrelevant links tend to be how we catch clever criminals, 'cause they assume it's something so small that it isn't even worth covering up."

"No, I don't know anything about the victim. But, the person who did it..." Alan gulped. Again, the words got stuck in his throat.

What was happening? What happened to all his conviction? Hadn't he been ready to turn the man in, no looking back? So, then, what was this, this sudden cowardice?

Maybe it's because there's so many cops here with me, he reasoned. *Or maybe it's because it's my first time making a report, so I don't know exactly what to say. Or...*

What if my intuition was right?

Yes, what if that primitive thing built into all people, the thing our old linguists decided to call 'instincts', had been correct all along. Could that little *part* of him really have known better than *him*?

Don't get the cops involved. You'll end up regretting it.

He could still see no reason behind that. No logical reason, at least. But now he could believe it. If Alan Michaels got the cops involved, Alan Michaels would not see the light of day again.

"The person who did it..." Alan began. "I don't know 'em." He could feel all eyes in the room boring into him. He began to feel a little light-headed. He groaned and brought a hand to his forehead. "I'm sorry, I think I should go."

And so Alan stood up and headed to the door. He tugged on the door as hard as he could, wholly oblivious to the calls of, "Sir, sir!" coming from behind him.

He managed to wrench the door open wide enough for him to squeeze through.

By the time he stood in the morning chill of the outside, his arms had gone awfully sore, and his conscience awfully heavy.

He began his shameful trek home, his eyes never leaving the ground. On one hand, he was upset with himself that he had not been able to just get the words out, get this whole thing over and done with.

But the part of him that was upset was, oddly, tiny. The rest of him was relieved that he hadn't followed through. He felt as though these other parts spoke to him, and what they said was this:

Alan Michaels, you are one lucky bastard!

Chapter 15

What a nightmare.

Following the whole debacle at the station, all Alan could do was heave a sigh, plow through the few miles that separated the police station from the comfort of his own home, climb into bed, and catch up on all the sleep he had missed on the previous night.

And this was the way things remained for several weeks, with Alan turning in late and waking even later. This behavior carried on for so long that, at some point, the snow on the window's ledge had given way to springtime sunlight.

So, if any of the regulars at Chloe's Café sat there wholly confused as to why balding Alan Michaels seemed never to be present recently (none of them noticed, apart from Chloe, who was currently in the kitchen grumbling to herself that she kept missing out on a morning sale), the reason was simple: The balding old man in question was always asleep at six in the morning, which was when he tended to wake up.

Seven? Nope, still out cold. Eight came and went, but Alan stayed unmoved. At nine in the morning, Nala woke up and was startled by his presence—his side of the bed was usually long since vacant by this time.

It was half past ten when Alan at last awoke, and that too was not of his own volition; The sun had risen high enough to stab into his eyes, and it was this unpleasantry that forced him up.

Alan grumbled and drew the curtains shut. For a long, bleary moment he considered going back to bed. But, no point. His kids were still here, so he needed to be a good role model.

He had a quick shower, stepped into a fresh set of clothes, put on his sweater, and into the kitchen he went.

Nala gave him a worried look as he entered. "Alan, are you feeling alright? You've woken so much later than usual the past few weeks. Is everything alright? Are you stressed about something?"

"What? No, no, I'm fine," he said, and even if he *had* been telling the truth, his tone would've had anyone sending him a look of suspicion. In fact, just to prove the point, Asher and Madison, who had been quietly tending to their breakfasts, had now turned to him, their brows lowered just the smallest amount.

Alan pretended not to notice. He grabbed a plate and got on with making himself a bit of breakfast.

His toast was just starting to turn golden brown when his children announced that they were done with their breakfasts. They got up, dropped their plates and cutlery in the sink, and off they went stomping into the living room.

Alan sighed. Even at this age, they couldn't wash up by themselves?

A whispered meeting between Alan's wife and kids took place in the living room. Perhaps they thought that the combination of their own whispering and the browning toast right by his ear would keep him out of the loop. It did for the most part, but an occasional word or two slipped through the cracks.

He heard an 'Alan' or a 'Dad' more than a couple of times. He hadn't thought much of it at first, but soon all that clandestine whispering began to annoy him. Throwing his name about while he wasn't there? What nonsense.

Some time had passed since the clock struck twelve. Alan, for the first time in forever, had opted to stay in; after all, the only writing he'd so far managed to do was done while he was at home. Perhaps all the bacon and toast and fantastic stories at the diner were not as conducive to his writing as he had first thought.

He was sitting in bed, editing what he'd so far written, when Madison poked her head shyly in at the door. Alan couldn't help but smile at how adorable she looked. However, as he soon realized, her expression of shyness was nothing more than a red herring.

"Dad?" she said, her voice sounding more excited than shy.

"Yes, Madison, what is it?" he said, setting his pencil down and closing the book.

"Me, Ash, and Mom have been talking about it, see, and we think you've seemed a little stressed out recently," she said.

"No, not really. My writing has been going pretty well recently, actually, so I don't kn—"

"So," she said a little loudly, informing him of the fact that it was a done deal and he had no say in the matter. "We've decided to go on a camping trip."

Alan cocked his head. "A camping trip? On such short notice? Are there any grounds that'll let us book in just a couple hours before the fact?"

Madison giggled. "Dad, you and Mom said the exact same thing. When we mention camping you instantly jump to a man-made campsite? No, Dad, we're going to wander through the forest with the butterflies and bees, and we're setting up camp at the first clearing we find."

"A-a forest?" Alan said, going a little pale. "You mean a *real* forest? With, like, bears and tigers and stuff?"

Madison burst into startled laughter. "Dad, we aren't going to the Amazon. There's a National Forest about twenty miles from where our college is. Me and Ash have always wanted to go on one of our weekends, just go and explore, really."

"Well, what stopped you?" Alan asked.

"Well, the idea of having to take a taxi twenty miles either way wasn't really attractive, but it was mostly that we were just flooded with assignments."

"Oh," he said. "And you two want to go there now?"

"Not we *two*," she said, "Us *four*. We're all going."

"Um..." Alan trailed off. "Can I opt out, by any chance?"

"Of course you can, Dad," she said, and the sweetness of her voice startled him. Then, just as sweetly she went on, "But if you don't come, I'll pout to the ends of the earth. You give me cake on my birthday, I'll eat it while pouting, and when Father's Day comes around, I'll give you a hug and a kiss while pouting."

Alan laughed. He went over to the door and hugged Madison, wringing another giggle out of her.

"Alright, I'll come. We're going today?"

"Yup, today. No clue when we'll arrive, though. If the traffic is anything like it was when we came home, we might only get there tomorrow."

"Gee, thanks for the confidence boost."

"You're most welcome, Dad," Madison said with a smile. "Now, you go sit down and relax for a bit, the three of us will get all the prep done and join you."

"No, it's alright, I'll hel—"

Madison poked him in the chest, a maternal sort of anger on her face. "Dad, we're doing this for *you*, so it's common sense that *you* should take it easy. Otherwise it'd be like you planning your own birthday party."

"But—"

"No buts!" she said, poking his chest once more. "Now, GO!"

Arguments were not going to lead anywhere, he realized, so he acquiesced. Out of the room he trotted. And as soon as he was sitting and relaxed, as reluctant as he was to admit it, he no longer felt like helping.

Nala came clambering out with several bags with tents in them. This startled Alan a little: He had never known they *had* a tent.

"Alan, would you mind popping the trunk?" Nala said.

"Huh? Oh, sure." He followed her out of the car, reached beyond the driver's seat, and pulled one of the little levers at the foot of the door. There was something like a thud from the back of the car.

"Thank you!"

Madison came a moment later with another disassembled tent—*Where are we getting all these tents?*—and into the trunk it went.

Soon, baskets of food, blankets, pillows, and a few other things filled the trunk to the brim... That was not an exaggeration. The three of them together could not get the trunk shut, so, as reluctant as they were to bother him, they had to solicit Alan's help. Even with the whole family going at it, it was by no means a cinch, but they got it done eventually.

Asher drove—Madison *wanted* to, but she was reminded by Asher of how she'd flunked four separate tests and was eventually forced to bribe the instructor into giving her a license. Blushing and grumbling, Madison sank into the back seat and said nothing more.

It'd been a hell of a long time since Alan had left town. A few years, at least, for his business never brought him there. The greenery and foliage they zoomed past were stunning. He remembered a time when *their* town had looked that green—but then home builders discovered chainsaws.

The trip must've lasted at least an hour, but Alan was aware of none of it. He'd been too busy gazing out the window with a look of awe, seeming in those moments an awful lot like a baby who had just discovered a new toy.

The car slowed and came to a stop at the side of an empty freeway. Alan only realized they had stopped when he noticed that the trees were no longer sailing past, but just standing there stagnant.

"Dad, we're here," Asher said.

"Oh. Oh, okay." Unsure of what he was expected to do, he undid his seatbelt and got out the car. He looked at the pines lining the perimeter of the forest, their leaves untouched by the winter—he assumed it was the forest, but he had no idea, really.

"Dad, sorry to bother you," Madison said, "but we need help getting stuff out of the trunk. Would you mind helping us carry some of it?"

Alan's eyes went a little wide. "You're getting *everything* out of the trunk?"

"No, no, of course not. Just the blankets, the tents, and enough food for a couple of meals. We won't really be needing even the pillows until night time."

"Oh. Alright."

Alan popped the trunk, and the four of them each found something to busy their arms with.

The parents carried the bags of tents, the youngest brought the blankets, and the eldest took the baskets and plates, but not before shutting the trunk, locking the car door, and shoving the keys deep inside his pocket.

They had been walking for several minutes when Alan, who was walking at the front, realized that he had no clue what he was even looking for.

"How much farther?" Alan called behind him.

"No clue," Asher called back. "But, if I stopped at the right spot, a couple of friends who have been here before said it should be just up ahead.

"*What* should be just up ahead?" Alan asked, suspense growing thick in his chest.

"Secret," Madison said mysteriously. "For now, just focus on the trail, Dad. Otherwise we'll get lost."

And focus he did. Soon the trees began to thin, so he didn't have to worry much anymore about snagging the tent on something. Farther down they got even thinner, and soon failed altogether. Alan stepped forward out of the last of the trees, his expression awed.

It was a sward, vast and empty. Overhead the boughs of evergreens kept off most of the light, and underfoot the clearing was carpeted with grass, yellowing at the tips but otherwise perfectly healthy.

Alan dropped the tent on the ground, took off his shoes, and headed for the center of the clearing. The grass felt ticklish in a comforting sort of way. It hadn't yet reached his lips, but Alan's heart was smiling.

He arrived at the perfect center of the clearing, and in a sea of rustles he lay down. His eyes he left gazing upwards. The sky was a little overcast, and he thought he could hear the distant rumbling of a brewing storm. But, who knows, maybe that was just his overly vivid imagination filling in the blanks.

Alan felt close to tears. It was wonderful. This was life. Not a best-selling book, and not a fantastic career with all the fame in the world, and neither yet a pay raise or a well-paid job.

No, none of that mattered. All Alan needed was *this*.

Alan was just beginning to doze off when he felt someone's body bumping into his own. It was Nala, coming to join him.

"Enjoying it so far?" she asked, her voice as soft as though she were speaking to her child.

Words did not come to him, so he nodded as best as he could with his head on the ground.

She ruffled his hair. "That's good. You were dozing off earlier, weren't you? If you're tired, it's fine if you want to tap out for a little."

"Nah, I'm alright," he said. He laced his fingers and stretched his arms into the air. "Just a little overwhelmed."

A sudden draught sent some of Nala's loose hair into her face. She set it behind her ear with a finger, then said, "Yeah, it's really pretty, isn't it."

"Mmm." He sat up and looked around. The tents had been put up, he noticed. But something was missing. "Hey, Nala?"

"Mmm?" she said, sounding just a couple seconds from dozing off herself.

"Where are the kids?"

"Hm? Oh, they went in a little deeper to explore. Their friend told them that there's a waterfall a little ways off, so they went to check it out."

"Oh." He thought for a moment about going and fetching them, but decided against it. "Well, as long as they're safe," he said, and he lay back on the grass.

Soon enough he found out that they were, in fact, safe. They came skipping back to the clearing, nearly shrieking in excitement.

"Dad! Mom! Come look," Asher said. "There *is* a waterfall over there!"

"Lord, it was so pretty," said, sounding touched. "It had little rainbows at the bottom and everything. And the sound, good God, the sound."

"Come see it, you two!"

"Mmm. Before we head home," Nala said, and immediately the pair looked like two balloons being deflated. "For now, though," Nala went on, and the way she said it made them perk right back up. "Come join us, you two. It's family time."

They came over at once. Asher lay next to his mother, and Madison, perhaps not quite understanding that she was now in her twenties, lay right on top of her father.

"Oh God, so heavy," he breathed without willing.

"Rude." Madison said, but she was smiling at him with the same eyes she had had when she was a baby, and all he could do at the sight of them was plant a kiss on her cheek and rest a gentle hand on her head.

Alan and Nala had been close to dozing off, but the prospect of sleep disappeared from their minds as soon as these two had joined in.

The kids talked, and talked, and talked, until eventually their parents shared a tired look and a wry smile before joining in.

They talked of college, and old wives' tales, and how writing was going (as Alan was proud to learn, Asher was working on a novel himself). Laughs and kisses and playful swats were shared, and within an hour, they were all too tired to wring even another sentence out of themselves. In spite of the pair of perfectly healthy tents standing proud at the edge of the clearing, the quartet fell into their slumbers right there on the yellow grass.

Just before Alan had fully been whisked away to sleep, with a pleasant smile on his face, he found one last thought wriggle its way into his mind:

Yes, this is it.

Chapter 16

Alan's internal clock had been as much a mess as he had been over the last couple days, but today it had righted itself. Right as the clocks back in civilization would have been striking six, Alan awoke.

And for the first time in God knew how long, his awakening was met with a big lump of thoughtless silence in his head; on another day, his thoughts right after waking would look something like this:

The book, the book, need to work on the book—when is my next talk with the murderer again?—is Nala starting to suspect, I wonder, maybe I should come clean, maybe I should cook up something for the kids, surprise them, but they might not like it, I don't remember if Nala asked me to wake her but maybe she did, hopefully she doesn't miss an appointment because of me, did I have an appointment myself, oh God I hope—

Today, there was none of that.

Perhaps this was what he'd needed all this time: not a bed or a hot shower or a Diner, but an ocean of soil and grass beneath him, and the wide open sky accepting his unrelenting gaze above him.

Madison's cheek rested against his. He smiled. His hand still sat atop her head, just where he had left it the night before.

She blinked herself awake. "Morning, Daddy," she said, her voice monotonous but somehow not losing its sweetness.

Madison sat up. She stretched, yawned aloud, and looked around. She seemed a little startled to see where they were, as though she'd forgotten all about this camping trip that had been *her* idea to begin with.Her eyes suddenly fell on the tents some ways away, and an annoyed look appeared on her face.

"Those weren't easy to put up you know," she grumbled. "What was the point of that whole struggle if you guys were just gonna use them as decorations?"

"Aww, don't be upset, Madison," Alan said, pinching her cheek.

Madison still seemed annoyed, but she had now moved on from the tents, instead throwing her gaze about the rest of the clearing in search of something else to grumble about. Soon enough she found it.

"What do we do about these things?" she asked, nodding towards the pair still asleep beside them. "Dad, why'd you wake the youngest first? Isn't it common knowledge that you're supposed to work your way *down*? I mean, just look at that!" she said, pointing at Nala. "That thing isn't in college. It doesn't need as much sleep as I do."

Alan laughed. What an absurd rant, and he had a front row seat to it.

"Madison," he said, letting slip a chuckle. "I'd appreciate it if you didn't talk about your Mom and big brother like they were sardines in a can. Also, your Mom does a lot of housework, so you can't blame her for being tired."

Madison didn't seem to be listening. She had instead found a small stick a couple feet from where they lay, and she was now using it to prod at her mother and brother.

The former was unsurprisingly unresponsive, but the latter started awake at once.

"God, whaddya want, Madison? I'm tired, lemme sleep a little more."

Poke. "Nope. I'm tired too, but I'm up, aren't I? *You're* the eldest, so shouldn't you be setting a good example for me?"

"I'm setting a good example by getting rest when I need it."

Poke. Poke, poke, poke.

"Alright, alright, I'm up, already!" Asher rubbed at his face, his hair in a fuzzy mess. "Geez, so early in the morning and you're already so pushy."

If Madison had heard that, she did a fantastic job at pretending she hadn't.

"Dad, you wake Mom." She handed him the stick, as though it were a necessity in the act of waking someone. "Mom always gets mad at us when we try and wake her."

"I don't need this," he said, setting the stick down, an action that seemed to disappoint Madison. He went up right beside his wife and began poking her in the ribs with his finger. "Nala. Hey, Nala, wake up. It's morning. The kids are awake, too."

There was a few seconds of silence, then a twitch before her eyes fluttered open. She yawned then said, "Morning, Alan, Asher, Madison."

"Good morning, Nala."

"Mornin', Mom."

"Sardine."

While Alan burst into a long, startled bout of laughter, Nala and Asher turned to Madison and stared as though she had an ear where her eye should've been. Well, of course they were confused; they had been asleep while Alan and Madison had been talking.

It took a long while, but Alan did eventually manage to compose himself.

"Ah, anyway," he said, wiping away a tear, "now that the family's all up, it's time to go."

Asher looked more than a little disappointed. "What? So soon, Dad? I thought the plan was to go home tonight. We packed as much as we did assuming as much."

"Ah, no, no, Asher, not home," Alan said. "You two said you'd found a waterfall, right? Well, come on. Let's go see it."

It was as though a pair of Christmas lights had just lit up the early morning dawn of the clearing, such was their happiness at hearing those words.

They hopped to their feet like a pair of rabbits. The eldest took his mother's hand, the youngest her father's entire arm.

They ventured into the deeper parts of the forest, and Alan felt as though he were a grain of sand in an hourglass. The clearing they had occupied had been treeless. As they stepped deeper into the forest, the trees took up more and more of the ground, but then eventually began to thin again.

At the end of this thinning lay another clearing, except this was not one of grass, but stone.

It *was* beautiful. Mesmerizingly so. The sound of it, had it been man-made, would've sounded terribly unpleasant. But this was *not* something man-made, but one of nature's own creations.

"Can we go play in it?" Madison asked, sounding a lot more like a five year old than a business major.

"Did you bring a swimsuit?" Alan asked.

"Um... No, not really." She looked to the side, finding a suitable alternative. "Can't I just go in, then let my clothes dry after?"

"Madison, winter just ended. Your clothes *won't* dry with the temperature being what it is."

She grumbled, but after a short bit of wheedling, Nala and Alan decided she could leave her feet in the water.

So she trotted over to the edge of the waterfall, rolled her jeans up, sat down on the edge, and set her feet into the water. She hadn't been peddling with her feet for two minutes, the happiest little smile you could imagine upon her face, when Asher joined her.

Alan and Nala were leaning against opposite sides of a tree, watching the two of them, and, as he took in the smiles they wore, Alan found himself wishing that this moment would never end.

But of course, it had to. They stayed for so long that the sun began creeping its way up the sky, occasionally peeking in on their clearing through an opening in the leaves.

Soon the sun had risen so high that its image reflected on the surface of the water began to hurt his eyes.

"Alright, you two, I think that's enough for now."

There was no shortage of grumbling at the sound of those words. But, nonetheless, they were obedient children.

"Can we come back here some day?" Asher asked, barefoot with his shoes dangling from his fingertips.

"Of course we can. It's only an hour's drive, isn't it?" Alan said. "Also, why are you two rushing our departure? Wasn't the plan to leave at night?

"Yup!" said Madison.

Off she and Asher went to the car to get more food. When they returned, the four of them began to eat; Alan wasn't really all that hungry, but he wouldn't have liked for them to feel awkward.

The day wore on, and the kids explored, lay panting for a while, took a sip of water, went to their parents for a short talk, then explored some more.

The day went by quicker than any other, and Alan was a little sad when, many hours later, the sun had slipped all the way beneath the horizon, leaving just its scarlet echoes to keep them company.

Alan struggled to think up a way to breach the subject of leaving. But, there was no need.

"Alright!" said Madison, stretching and getting to her feet. "That's enough for today, I think. Come on, guys, lets pack up and go home." She gave Alan a teasing look out of the corner of her eye. "Or else the tigers and bears might turn up."

Alan and Nala took apart the tents while the kids moved the baskets and blankets back into the trunk. The tents joined them a moment later, and the family threw their entire collective weight onto the trunk, until at last it locked itself in place with a satisfying click.

And, it seemed, not a moment too soon. They had barely gotten the doors shut when the rain came, droplets the size of bullets crashing down onto the roof of the car.

Alan had to yell to make himself heard over the noise of the rain. "You sure you don't want me to drive?" he said to Asher.

"I'm fine, Dad!" he yelled back.

Dusk had settled in for real, and the rain, as it seemed to have a tendency of doing, was causing a traffic jam. And it was as such that they inched on home, rain pattering against the roof of the car and all the family filled with a pleasant languor.

They arrived home a couple hours or so later, and Asher had hardly pulled into the driveway when the back doors were thrown open as Nala and Madison rushed to get out. Alan and Asher shared a wry smile before disembarking themselves. They briefly discussed getting the luggage out of the trunk but decided against it. Too much work, too little left in the tank.

Asher rushed upstairs to his room, Madison to hers. Alan watched them go, a pleasant smile on his face, before going over to his own room. Nala was in the shower.

His eyes fell on his bed, and he sighed. Unlike the rest of the family, his day was not quite done yet. No. Now that he could think clearer, he decided that a confrontation was necessary. He needed to do it while the high of the trip was still thick in his body, otherwise the cowardice would set in, and his method of dealing with this issue would go from a true confrontation to merely prodding the *idea* of one with a ten foot pole.

Alan planted a pair of soft knocks on the bathroom door. "Hey, Nala?"

"Mm? What is it, Alan?" she said, a little startled.

"The rain's let up, and I'm not really in the mood to cook, so I'm going out to fetch something from town. Do you want anything?"

"Oh, no, no, that's alright. I'm heading straight to bed after my shower. I'm really not hungry anyway, so no need to worry about me."

"Alright, if you say so," Alan said. "I'll be back in a bit. Goodnight, Nala. Sweet dreams."

"Alright, thank you, Alan. You too."

And Alan was off. Not to town, of course, but to the payphones.

Were it a movie, all of the audience would've by now been egregiously familiar with what Alan's walks to the payphone tended to entail. As such, the journey itself shall go unmentioned.

His pace had improved remarkably from what it had been the first time. He could now do the entire journey in half the time without ever breaking a sweat, and what a good thing, too: Nala's suspicions were beginning to drain away, he could tell. Just a little longer, and she'd think nothing at all of his long stays at the 'diner'.

He arrived at the station at what he suspected would count as the fledgling moments of the 'cowardly hours'. *Cowardly?* he thought. A man braver than he would have quailed under this darkness. If he thought about the fact, he was sure he'd freeze up.

Alan threw open the door to the payphone—he'd *meant* to ease it open gently, as he had been doing on all his previous visits, but, with no frost on its hinges or snow on the ground, it welcomed him with no complaints at all (except, of course, the great groan it gave).

Alan punched in the number, leaned his back against the door, and waited. And waited. And waited...

Is he out or something?

After a minute or so, Alan began to grow just a tad impatient. He drummed his fingers on the glass wall of the booth, and his eyes began to wander. It wasn't long before they fell on something... odd.

For a second, Alan didn't know what he was looking at. The glass of the booth was patchy, and there was a little more light streaming through in some places than in others. Alan stared. The thought of the flashlight laying in the grass crashed into his mind. He could do with it right now, but did he have the guts to venture out in the dark, cross right over the restrooms, and stick his hand into that tall, dry patch that could've housed most anything? No, he didn't think he did. And so he kept staring, hoping his eyes would adjust sooner rather than later.

And then the answer struck him, as hard and sudden as a rock thrown from the edge of a cliff. It was a terribly simple answer, but it nonetheless sent his blood curdling like the foam of an icy waterfall.

There was something smeared on the glass.

Alan didn't care what the substance was. For the first time throughout this whole ordeal, Alan felt true, unbridled fear.

Someone else has been here.

That was it. It had to have been. Of course, things did not smear unless *someone* smeared them.

Before Alan could get any further, however, a voice appeared on the line.

"What're you doing out here?" snarled the murderer. "Why ain't you in a sewer somewhere?"

"A-A sewer?" Alan stammered.

"Yeah, that's where you live, isn't it, you damned rat."

Alan's heart felt as though it was falling out of his feet. Alan knew just what he meant, but decided to pretend he did not.

"I don't understand. Why am I a rat?"

"You know exactly why. Try to snitch on me, you damn rat? Went to the police and froze up, didn't you? The nerve of you, trying and outing the man that'll put your lousy career back on track."

"How do you know all this?" Alan asked, and the lack of calm in his voice surprised even himself.

"Don't ask me how I know things. For the tenth time, I'm closer than you think I am." The man stopped to breathe, then chuckled darkly. "You know, I've never seen someone half as lucky as you."

"What do you mean?"

"The police. You froze up. I know you did. And a damn good thing for *both* of us."

"Sorry, I'm a little lost now. How is *you* not getting outed good for *me*?" asked Alan.

"Why? Simple. Because..." He paused, perhaps to give Alan a moment to brace himself. "I've planted evidence. Incriminating, undeniable evidence. Mostly your hair, but not *only*. A little bit of your sweat, some of your scent so the K9s don't get left out."

Alan blacked out. He was lucky he was leaning, for all that happened was that he slid down into a crouch.

"H-how did you get my hair?" said Alan, his voice trembling. "My sweat, how? I don't understand."

The murderer gave a long, hearty laugh, as though Alan's reaction truly amused him.

"Don't worry. I did that only as a precaution. Just in case you tried something funny like this. The evidence I planted? It's not *at* the scene of the crime itself. It's just somewhere close by, somewhere they wouldn't ever check.

"But," the man said, his voice going low and dangerous. "Try and pull that crap one more time, and the cops *may* just get a little tip-off, you know?"

Chapter 17

Alan hung up; did he put the phone down right after those words? Did Alan have something to say following the fact? Or maybe the conversation went on unperturbed, with Alan being unaffected by the murderer's words. Alan could not remember.

All he knew was that one second he was staring at the payphone, staring but not seeing, as though he were a corpse, and the next second he was turning the knob to his own front door. Where did all the miles in between go? Neither he nor his feet knew.

If Alan had to hazard a guess, he would've guessed it to be about one in the morning. The moon was blocked out by storm clouds, so he couldn't quite tell.

Nala was asleep. Alan hardly noticed. He got slowly into bed, pulled the covers over his head, and, in the midst of lamenting the fact that there was no chance at all of him catching any sleep tonight, he fell asleep.

And then morning was at his doorstep. Birds sat on the windowsill giving great, hearty chirps, and the eccentric a street down who for some reason owned a rooster decided to let it have free reign over the dawn.

Alan got up, stretched, took a quick shower, threw on his clothes, and, without being aware of having done any of this, he was off to the diner.

"Mornin', Chloe." He went over to his usual seat and was about to sit down, but then he paused. He turned his gaze to a different table, one close to the center of the establishment and not so cut off from the rest of the world. Alan looked between the two tables a few times, shrugged, and then made for the one in the center; perhaps something as simple as a change of perspective would be enough to do something for him. He was unsure what that something was, but, truthfully, he'd take anything.

"Morning, Alan," Chloe said, surely glad that one of her cash cows had returned after a short stint away. "So, what'll it be? The usual?"

Alan cocked his head. "How come you're *asking* today? You usually just go in the back and prepare it."

"Yup," she said, "and *you* usually sit in that corner over there." She nodded toward the table in question. "You seemed to be keen on an adventure today, so I thought I'd ask. So, what fits the bill?" She looked off into space for a moment. Alan couldn't tell if it she was in genuine thought, or if she was merely teasing him. "Oh! I got it!" she said suddenly. "What about you eat your toast *with* the crust for once, instead of having me remove it like you're some sort of child?"

Alan felt himself blush. "Toast with crust is the worst. It scrapes the roof of your mouth."

"Oh, does it?" Chloe said. "I don't eat toast, so I wouldn't know."

"Yes, yes. Now," Alan said, waving her away, "go prepare my breakfast. You kids, I swear, you get distracted so easily."

Chloe laughed, then headed on over to the kitchen. Alan took the opportunity to look around, and he couldn't help but notice how strange the diner looked; he could see everyone, and everyone could see him. It was an odd feeling, but he didn't dislike it.

Just as Alan was philosophizing about how just the smallest of changes in perspective was enough to make the most familiar of things seem so foreign, Chloe came up with his breakfast.

"There we are," she said as she set the plate down. She wiped her hands on her apron, then threw her gaze about the room, a satisfied look on her face. "Everyone served, no tinkles in the last twenty minutes. How wonderful."

"Doesn't that just mean business is bad?" Alan teased.

"No, it most certainly does not. It just means that everyone who wants feeding has been fed. Also, it's not like I've got anyone helping me. I'd love for the place to see a dry patch or two a day, 'cause that's the only time I can ever get any rest."

"Well, now you've got the chance, better not waste it on some old balding guy."

"Hmmm. Well, guess I'll let you enjoy your breakfast. In the meantime," she said, casting a nasty little grin at the pair of men at the counter, "I wonder what sort of stories those two have cooked up."

Chloe slipped away to go and bother Gus and Red, leaving Alan to tend to his breakfast, which he did one-handed; with his left hand he busied himself with penning down new chapters in his book. He hadn't been told anything new in the form of murders, but Alan still felt as though the other developments in this whole ordeal deserved a chapter or two in their own right.

His multitasking was going exceptionally well for a while, but something that fell on his ears caused both his hands to freeze at once.

"Gus, you did not *see* a murder. You *imagined* one," Chloe was saying.

It was as though those words were a fork of lightning, Alan a block of solid steel. He felt every nerve in his body come alight. His eggs slipped off the fork, but he didn't notice.

"I saw it, I tell you! I'm not kidding! I saw it."

Chloe closed her eyes and sighed. "Gus, you said this happened when?"

"Well..." Gus said, fidgeting more than a little. "Um... Well, a while ago."

"And you didn't divulge this information prior to this why, exactly?"

"I'll knock you over the head with your own frying pan and see how well *you* remember things after," Gus said.

Chloe laughed. "Fair enough." She allowed herself a few small chuckles, then leant in and lowered her voice. Alan had to strain his ears to listen. "So, you saw it *happen*? As in, you were there in the flesh, watching?"

"That's what I told you, girl. I wasn't even well-hidden, either. Just turned a corner, walked in on it, and froze right there in plain sight." He stuck his lower lip out and shook his head. "Guy didn't notice jack. Was too busy sawing the girl's limbs off." He shivered. "The screams she gave. Lord, you'd have thought... Well, you'd have thought she was having done to her exactly what *was* being done to her."

"And what about the guy who did it? You caught a glimpse of him? You informed the police?"

Red nodded importantly. "You bet we did." He looked off to the side, a thoughtful look appearing on his face. "I meant that we saw him, not that we informed the cops."

"You were there, Red?" Chloe asked, her eyes narrowed in confusion.

"You bet I was."

"So why haven't you been saying anything all this time?"

"Well, Gus is saying it, isn't he? Or, what, do you kids need two people for each story, one for each ear?"

Chloe grumbled. "You mean you saw all this, and you decided to share it with somebody who runs a restaurant instead of an actual cop?"

Gus took a long, long draught of his coffee. He cleared his throat importantly. "It's a diner. Also, we want to go report this, of course. We're just worried if the cops ask the same things as you. 'Why didn't you report this earlier?' and stuff like that. Seems like a hassle."

"You remember the guy's face?"

"I do, yes," Gus said.

"You mean *we* do, don't you, Gus?" said Red.

"Well, see, I'm privy to what knowledge I do and do not have, so I can say for sure whether something is within or without my knowledge. But you aren't me, so I don't kn—"

"Whoa, there, calm it, Plato," said Chloe.

"You asked!"

"I asked for the guy's description, not for you to start philosophizing."

"O-Oh. Of course. The description." Gus cleared his throat and dropped his voice a notch further. By this point, Alan had stopped even pretending to be minding his own business. He was staring right at the three of them, his ears perked like a puppy who had just caught the sound of his favorite toy. "I'll tell you what the guy looked like, hair for hair: to begin with, he didn't have much."

"Much what?"

Gus snarled. "Hair, girl, hair. Now you've forced me to dissect it, the joke's stopped being funny anymore."

"It never started being funny," Chloe said dryly, a hint of impatience creeping into her tone. "The description, get on with it, please. I'm dying of suspense over here."

"Like I said, he didn't have much hair. A big bald patch near the center of his scalp. His eyes were blue; I remember looking right into them and hoping they didn't turn to me. He was pretty tall, but not overly so. Same with his width. A *little* over what I would call average, but I think I only noticed because I was staring so hard. He kept a straight face, completely, not a hint of a smile or remorse or disgust or anything. It was a little creepy, really; it felt like he had just stolen a face from the morgue and sewed it over his own. He had a little bit of stubble, and his side burns ran all the way down to it."

Gus stopped for a moment and began to drum a single finger against his chin. "What else, what else..." Suddenly his finger stopped, and his face lit up. "I remember now!" he said, nearly rising to his feet in his excitement. "His hand, it had all these scars, as deep as valleys!"

Alan felt himself sink a little lower in his chair. He felt terribly numb, but he still found the energy to do one single thing: raise his left hand, stare at it. Scars, all as deep as valleys. He brought the same hand to his chin and gently stroked it. His stubble usually felt good on his fingertips, but today it felt like nothing in particular.

All of a sudden, Alan felt naked. What the hell was Gus talking about? Had Alan slighted him in some way without realizing it? Could this have been some sort of sick retribution? Or was his dementia truly that bad?

All eyes were on him. He knew they were. He raised his eyes, preparing himself for the sight of a dozen sets of curious orbs boring into him, politely demanding an explanation.

But what met him startled him perhaps even more. *Nobody* was looking at him. Not a single person.

Are these people deaf? Did they not hear what Gus just said? Or maybe they're blind and can't see me?

To an extent, it disappointed him. Dementia-stricken or not, someone had just offered up a description of what could've well been a murderer. Somebody of that exact description was in that very room. And yet, not one damn person batted an eyelid.

Alan glided his eyes across the room, as though he were afraid that darting them would result in his being noticed. Nobody, not one person...

A second later, Alan realized it wasn't true. His heart gave a great jump as his eyes happened upon another pair, a pair that was looking right at him. They were Chloe's.

The two considered each other for a long moment. Then Chloe turned away, rubbed at her forehead, and sighed.

"Hey, Gus." Her voice sounded tired all of a sudden. "You know, that description seems *awfully* familiar, doesn't it?"

Alan's heart gave another jump. Did she actually believe this nonsense?

"Whaddya mean? You know the guy?"

"Gus, I can tell you, you've just described someone, alright. You've described someone who's in here right now."

Gus' face went pale and stricken. "Wait, you mean..."

"Gus, you've just described Alan."

Gus seemed confused about this for a second. "What?"

"I said, you haven't described any murderers here. You've just described Alan. You see him every day, so I guess you're just filling in the blanks with someone familiar."

"Oh." Gus turned to Alan for a second, considering him, before turning back to Chloe. "It's just a coincidence. I'm sure of what I saw!"

Red set his mug down with a big thump. "You're wrong, Gus."

"What? Which part is wrong?"

"The scars. They were on his *face*, not his hand."

"No they weren't!"

"Also, his eyes were green, not blue."

"No, they were..." Gus sank into thoughtful silence. "Actually, you might be right about that."

"Of course. Also, it was a goatee."

"I'm putting my foot down on that, Red. It was handlebars. I'm sure of it."

Chloe held her head in her hands and shook it. "But... But you just said he had stubble?"

"Stubble? Why would I say he had stubble when he had handlebars?"

"Goatee," Red put in.

"No. Also, I just realized, we couldn't have possibly seen his eyes. His bangs went over them."

Chloe sputtered before managing to get out, "But you said he was bald?"

"Oh come now, Chloe. You're just making stuff up now."

"*I'm* making stuff up?!" said Chloe.

Alan let slip a small laugh. He felt relieved. Relieved from *what*, he couldn't tell you. Of *course* Gus was wrong. Like hell he'd caught Alan—*Alan*, of all people!—in the act of murdering someone. Alan was simply not thinking straight. If he'd had his head screwed on the right way, he'd have found this whole thing amusing. He would not have felt fearful, for he would have known that he, Alan Michaels, was no murderer.

He was at most an unwilling accomplice.

Alan picked up his fork and his pencil, chuckling to himself a tiny bit. As the discarded egg from earlier at last arrived at its destination, Alan smiled. His eyes found their way to the window, where they spied myriad of color; spring was here, well and truly.

The autumn had seemed to simply go on and on, what with all his talks with murderers and new ideas for books. But for all the promise the fall had shown, the winter was disappointing, to say the least.

As Alan eyed the budded flowers of spring, some not quite blooming just yet, he found himself wishing for the season to do to his life just what it did to those flowers: add a little color, make things just a little more appealing.

With that idea on the foreground of his mind, Alan set down his pencil with a click: another chapter was done.

Chapter 18

The short, fat hand of the clock struck two, and the second hand had not managed to tick sixty more times before Alan awoke. He felt a dull ache in his bones, and for a moment he was surprised to see trees not bare when he looked out the window—why, it's no longer winter! No, it was just the chill of the morning air that sent his muscles squeezing in on themselves.

The cowardly hours.

Alan snuck a glance at Nala: asleep, to the surprise of no one. With his eyes stuck to her like a nail on a board, he threw the covers back and got out of bed. He opened his door, shut it behind him, then stood in the hallway for a long, long moment. He was considering a myriad of different things, some more logical than others.

For instance, he thought about going upstairs to pay his kids a quick visit. It was not *necessary*, per se, but neither yet was there anything wrong with it.

For some reason, he felt an irresistible urge to leave through the window instead of the perfectly healthy front door. He stared at the window for a moment, tempted. Determined not to let his intrusive thoughts win, he turned away, opened the door, and out he went.

As he walked in the dark chill of the two a.m. world, he thought about the possibilities: Why would Gus' description have been a perfect copy of Alan?

One possibility was that the murderer was trying to frame him. Yes; he had known how many fingers he'd had behind his back, and he'd known all about why he hadn't called at Christmas. And when Alan had tried to turn him in? Of course, he had known about that too. It was not at all far-fetched to think he had cooked up a disguise to try and do Alan in.

The reasoning behind it, however, was lost on Alan. Revenge for trying to turn him in? No, it couldn't have been. This murder had happened before that attempt. Maybe the murderer simply disliked Alan, and was now doing what he could to be rid of him.

But the logic on that didn't quite go full circle either. If doing Alan in was truly his intention, there were two much easier ways to go about that: the first, he was a full-fledged murderer, for crying out loud, and he must've known that Alan made those calls from that devoid-of-life station. Walk in, slice, walk out, and no one in that whole damn town would be any the wiser.

The second way was much, much, simpler: just don't pick up the phone.

If nothing else held any credibility, the possibility that Gus' dementia was behind that description could not be ignored.

Regardless, here he was at the station, dark and decrepit as always.

As he approached the payphones, Alan felt a sudden nervous tingle; he had been having a strange feeling for a while now, but it hadn't sunk in until this very moment: This would be the last call. He could feel it in his heart of hearts, that, one way or another, his connection with this man was ending tonight.

His heart thumping in an odd rhythm, Alan punched in the number. Despite not having set up a talk in advance, the answer came in an instant.

"Hello, Alan."

The fact that this man knew Alan's name did not surprise him, though it did sound a little alien coming out of that mouth.

"Yes, hello." Alan's voice was calm. Eerily so. "Out of curiosity, how long have you known my identity, exactly?"

"How long?" A low, drawn-out chuckle ensued. "Alan Michaels, you're the only writer in this town who's worth a damn. You're also quite possibly the most famous person in the history of the town, so it should not surprise you if I said that I'd known about you long, long before we met."

Alan held his silence. He was ashamed. Ashamed that the words of a cold-blooded killer could flatter him so.

"What is it, Michaels? Cat got your tongue?"

"Oh, no. I don't have anything of note to add."

"You, Alan Michaels, an all-time great, a linguistic phenom, a mastermind of the literary arts, have nothing to add?"

His praise struck Alan in an odd way; it sounded so... so... *genuine.* It was as though he truly, honestly cared about Alan and his literary exploits.

Alan shook his head, thinking to himself, *No, this is the last. Don't develop some kind of Stockholm syndrome now, Alan.*

"Thank you for your kind words, but they're lost on me these days. I... Well, something happened about a year ago, and my writing has never quite recovered."

"Yeah? Well, damn. That's tough."

"A-Are you sympathizing with me?"

"Hm? Yes, I am, how nice of you for noticing." The man scoffed. "You have some misconceptions about my type, I think. First, you would probably ascribe words like 'cold-blooded' and 'ruthless' to me, wouldn't you? Unfair. I'm no more cold-blooded than anyone else. Everyone has their hobbies. Most are just lucky that theirs fall in that very wide spectrum of being both highly accessible *and* highly legal. *My* hobbies? Accessible, alright. But the legality of it? Present, so long as you avoid getting caught."

"That's not how it works," Alan said dryly. If he was certain this was the last meeting, why not say it as it was?

"Yes, yes. I'm sure you know all there is to know about most things, so I see no point in arguing with you. However," the man said, then allowed a short bout of silence to settle in. "I have to thank you, Michaels. For some time, I'd just been a cog in the clockwork. Now, I'm back to being the rust, and there's no better rust God's clock will ever see."

Alan had nothing to add. After a moment of silence, the man cleared his throat and began speaking again.

"Your book, you're hoping to finish it soon, aren't you? Most of it's already penned down, isn't it?" Without allowing Alan to reply, he went on, "That's good. I had no intention of dragging this out any further."

Alan lowered his brows in confusion. "I don't think I follow. What do you mean, you didn't want to drag it out?"

"I meant just what I said. This whole thing, you, me, your book—I wish to get it over and done with."

Suddenly Alan felt a terrible shiver; an image of the murderer's face appeared in his mind, split into a wide, maniacal grin.

"And," the murderer went on, the tone of his voice turning every bone—every *cell*—in Alan's body into a shriveled mess. "Since the book is nearing its completion, I thought to myself, 'Hey, why not go out with a bang?'"

Alan had a sudden urge to hang up. Hang up, walk away from the station, cast his book into the fire, and forever hold his peace.

And he truly *did* attempt to hang up. But something kept his hand from pulling away, kept the phone as firm as rock against his ear, so that every word the murderer said sounded as crisp and clear as if a trumpet had blown not ten feet off.

"Go out with a bang, meaning what?" Alan asked, failing to mask the quiver in his voice. "Y-You're not planning an actual bombing, or some kind of genocide, I hope?"

"Genocide?" The man snorted derisively. "There aren't any demographics that I have enough collective hatred for to go through the trouble of planning something like that. As for the bombing... You've been watching too many cop shows. Too many bad ones, at least. You know, the kind where the bad guys have a meeting in the basement where they plan to rob some bank. They go in with hardly any semblance of a proper plan, shoot some blanks into the air, then hold the room hostage. Cops turn up, these guys don't know what to do, and all of a sudden one of these fools Mickey Mouse a stick of dynamite out of their damn pants." The man laughed long and hard. When the murderer at last stopped laughing some time later, he was still breathing a little hard. "Anyway, point is, explosives aren't that easy to acquire. Arms? Arms are easier to get. This is all word of mouth though, so take it with a tablespoon of salt. I've never actually hazarded an attempt at acquiring either."

"Alright," Alan said, a little relieved that the two worst options were out of the way. "So what did you mean when you said you wanted to go out with a bang?"

"Here's a hint, Michaels: only *you* would be able to see the bang in it. No one else would give a damn."

A terrible thought appeared in Alan's mind. "You're going to kill... me?"

"Good guess. But, incorrect. Firstly, killing you would get pretty complicated pretty quickly. Couldn't tell you why that is, so you'll just have to take my word for it. And secondly: Alan Michaels, I'm not that banal. I choose my victims as carefully as a director chooses his actors. I don't just step outside and take a swipe at the first person I see."

A long moment of silence fell between them. It seemed to grow and expand like smoke in the sky, and soon it had grown so thick that Alan was afraid to break the silence.

The murderer spoke first. "So, any other guesses as to what my grand finale entails? Or shall I give you one more small clue?"

"Um..." Alan had no idea how he was meant to play this anymore. Never before had he lost control of a conversation this badly. "Yes, a clue would help. Yes."

"First of all, I assume you've figured out the little game I've been playing with you?"

Alan nodded, certain that the murderer could see it. "You've been telling me about future murders, not past ones."

The man snapped his fingers. "Bingo. Now, you remember how I've been telling you to pick a number between one and three, one and two, whatever? Well, now we're down to one. The bang. I have to say, the last two times you missed her, I was not pleased. But now, now that there's no other tracks for the train to turn onto, I'm glad it happened this way. Really, I am. It would've been a horribly short book if you'd landed on her on the first attempt."

Alan was not listening. He *couldn't* listen. A single word had caused him to freeze. His heart stopped; his knees seemed an inch from giving way; his breath caught in his throat, and there it stayed for the longest time.

Her.

Alan had a sinking feeling he knew who the murderer was talking about. Alan's mouth opened and closed a few times, trying to get the question out, but it refused to leave his throat.

"Michaels, you're a clever man, aren't you? Tell me the truth: this meeting, you *knew* it would be the last, didn't you?"

A long, long silence ensued. After what could not have been less than an entire minute, Alan at last found his voice.

"I did."

"Of course. Your instincts are sublime, Michaels. I'll give you that, if nothing else."

Alan cleared his throat. This constant going off on tangents had gone on long enough. "So," he said, "this bang you're talking about, what does it entail, exactly?"

"You know, I'm sure. I could feel it in you. As soon as I mentioned that word, you figured it out."

Alan shivered terribly. The urge to hang up was gone; now he just wanted to drop the phone and run. Run, grab his family, toss them into the back seat, and drive over as many national borders as he could without landing them all in the ocean.

The murderer chuckled. "A good reaction. Not the greatest I've ever drawn out of someone, but not too shabby. A modest, let's say, six out of ten." There was a short pause, then the man's voice became softer. It sounded close to pity. "You brought this on yourself, you know."

"How?" Alan yelled into the phone. "How is any of this my fault?"

"You, Michaels—you're indecisive. You want your cake and to eat it too. You want the family of a normal man, but the career, the lifestyle, of a bohemian." The man clicked his tongue several times, as though he were calling over a cat. "That's not how life goes, Michaels. You can have one or the other, and that's it. Don't believe me? Just look. You *had* both, then that accident came, and you were forced to part with one of them."

"My career was a train wreck even before the accident," Alan said. He was only putting in things of his own as something of a defense mechanism, a way to distance himself from the grand revelation; the 'bang', Alan already knew what it was. The ice in his stomach had told him.

But it was no use; the murderer seemed to know what Alan was doing.

"Yeah? That's just the way the cookie crumbles, Michaels. You know, I've found it quite the remarkable thing. The way your names are just the other's in reverse. Glue 'em together any way you like, you've got a palindrome."

Alan could hear the maniacal grin in the murderer's voice when he spoke.

"But, a palindrome it will be no longer."

Alan shook his head.

Don't say it.

"Alan Michaels, it's been a good half-year. But—"

Don't say it.

"—now, it all comes to a close. Michaels, I hope you left a good few pages blank, because for the closing act, the grand finale—"

Please, don't say it!

"—your other half, Nala Michaels, will be finding her way into that book."

Chapter 19

Alan slammed the phone down, the force of it causing his insides to vibrate like the tines of a tuning fork.

He threw open the door of the booth and ran. He ran faster than he'd ever ran before. In his panic and desperation, the idea of flagging down a cab did not for a moment occur to him.

He ran, and he stumbled, and he fell, and he got back up, and he kept running. But it kept happening. He kept stumbling and tripping over nothing. It was as though his legs had lost their autonomy and would only function under very clear instructions from Alan's fried, frazzled brain.

By the time he had turned the corner onto his street, he had made a worse time than if he'd simply walked.

Knees torn and bleeding, lungs straining, heart thumping, Alan threw open the front door.

There was Nala. A bloody heap on the floor, eyes wide and staring. Staring, but not seeing. The walls were red, and the world seemed to be spinning. Alan fell to his knees beside his wife, and he stared into her eyes, knowing full well she would never return his gaze...

That was what Alan had been expecting to walk in on.

But reality stunned him far worse, for there was none of that. The walls were their usual blue, the floors white and gleaming like polished marble.

No, nothing out of the ordinary. Except, of course, for the three people on the couch, all staring at him startled, like a family of deer who had just been thrust into a pair of headlights.

"Nala," Alan said, a clear quiver to his voice. "You're... You're..."

You're alive? he wanted to say. But that would have sounded more than a touch odd. In fact, it was hard to take it as anything but a threat. As though he'd hired a hitman, and was now surprised that the job was still pending. And then he'd have to explain all about what he'd been up to these past six months; where he had taken all of Nala's trust and dumped it.

In the end, he opted to go down a different route.

"Why are you all up so late?" He shook back his sleeve and eyed his watch. "It's past three in the morning. Why aren't you guys in bed?"

He caught Nala and Asher sharing an odd look. Madison, on the other hand, ignored the question altogether.

"Dad, you alright?" she asked. She was standing right beside him with her hands on his shoulders, but he hadn't noticed her getting up. "You're out of breath, Dad. Please, come, sit down."

"I'm fine."

He lifted her hands gently off his shoulders. She offered no resistance, but eyed him with a look that was an odd mix of concern, pity, and anger. But Alan did not notice. He was too busy staring at Nala.

"Dad, you're not fine. Not at all. I wouldn't need to be your daughter to see that."

She gave him a long, searching look, and when next she spoke, her words caused Nala to flinch terribly.

"You... haven't been drinking, have you?"

"Drinking?" Alan cocked his head in genuine confusion. "Why would I have been drinking? You know I don't drink."

"You're not fine!" Madison said, her tone agitated. For a long moment the pair simply eyed each other, and she seemed surprised to see his eyes filled with innocence. When Madison at last broke the silence, her voice had gone low, and even a little dangerous.

"You mean you don't remember any of that? Everything you put Mom and us through? All the anger and beatings you had us take when you were drunk; You don't remember?"

Alan had gone pale. "B-beatings? Me?" he said, his heart hammering as though in denial. He looked at each of them in turn. "When would I have beaten any of you?" As though attempting to convince himself rather than anyone else, Alan went on in hardly more than a whisper: "It can't be true... No, it can't be. Yes, yes. They're just making it up..."

"We aren't." It was Asher this time. The sound of his voice made Alan cower a small bit. It was low and stern, a tone Madison's puppy voice could only dream of. "Dad, it's all true. Maybe the accident made you forget, but all of what Madison said happened." He shrugged. "Guess even your accident has a silver lining." He sent Alan a look, colder than the winter they'd just left behind. "It was your fault, you know. You were driving drunk and somehow ended up going against the traffic. *You* killed that guy. But, of course, the town just swept the whole thing under the rug. You were worth too much to them. Too rich and famous. They couldn't let the news out, that their cash cow had just committed manslaughter. Where would all their revenue go?"

"Asher!" Nala chided. Then, just as suddenly she said, "Alan?" Alan flinched. He hadn't been expecting her to speak. "Why do you keep staring at me? What is it?"

"O-Oh," Alan stammered. He shook his head to clear it, and he shifted his eyes, suddenly feeling a little self-conscious. "N-No, it's nothing, Nala. I had a really bad nightmare, is all."

Nala narrowed her eyes. She didn't believe him. Despite that, however, rather oddly, Alan was put at ease by the fact. But, then again, perhaps that sudden calm was caused by the fact that she was still alive rather than anything else.

Alan stepped forward. As he made his way across the room, three pairs of eyes stared at him, each a mix of emotions difficult to pen down.

Alan walked up to his wife, lifted her off the couch and up to her feet, wrapped his arms around her waist, and rested his head on her shoulder.

"Nala," he said softly. "I had a bad dream."

She seemed a little confused by this, but she returned his hug nonetheless, occasionally stealing a perplexed glance at one of her children.

It was a long moment before she broke the silence.

"Yes, Alan, I heard," she said, her voice soft and maternal. "Do you feel like talking about it?"

"I really don't want to talk about it." Alan opened his mouth to say more, paused, then closed it again. This happened a few more times.

"You have something to say, don't you? Go ahead and say it. I won't mind."

"It was about you, Nala," he said, and his voice was filled with so much conviction that even Alan forgot that it was a lie. "Something bad happened to you in that dream. I'm scared, Nala, because what if it happens for real? What am I supposed to do then?"

"So, you mean to tell me that you're a little paranoid now, Alan?"

Alan shook his head. "Not a little. A lot." He pulled away from her a small bit, just enough to look her in the eyes. "Nala, I'm sorry, but for my sake, could you please do something for me?"

"What's that, Alan?"

"For just a week... Um, maybe two, would you mind not leaving the house?"

Nala laughed. "Well, I rarely leave the house anyway. But the grocery shopping will have to be done by someone."

"I'll do it," Alan said quickly. "I promise I'll take care of it, so you just stay home, alright, Nala?"

"Of course, of course." Nala gave a cheeky smile. "Why, I'll have to thank that brain of yours for cooking up that dream. Now I can have a whole week off."

"Dad," Madison said. "You've still got the shakes. I think you should lie down." She grinned playfully, then made a show of sniffing at him. "And, maybe a shower while you're at it."

Alan's heart was still twanging uncomfortably, and his thoughts were still so messy that even he was struggling to decipher them. And yet, that little action of Madison's seemed to bring a little light back into his life. Bright did not mean calm, but he couldn't help but smile.

"Yes, Madison, you're right." He went over to their room and stepped inside, and in the split second right before he shut the door, he cast Nala a final, rueful look over his shoulder, as though he truly feared that it may have been the last.

He decided to run himself a bath. He tended not to have the patience for it, but today was different. Today, he was in a terrible, terrible panic, but it manifested itself in very odd ways, and this was just one of them.

Alan hummed to himself while he soaked away in the tub. He looked out the skylight, and he couldn't help feeling a little jealous. Jealous of everything *outthere*. The birds, the only thought running through their heads being that of when their next scheduled worm would be.

Alan closed his eyes and sighed. Not only did the action wholly fail to calm him, it in fact aggravated him further.

You brought it upon yourself.

Alan sank a little lower into the tub. "How?!" he yelled, but with his mouth submerged it sounded closer to a gargle than anything else.

A half-hour later, Alan drained the tub and set about finding a fresh set of clothes. He put his shirt on backwards, clicked his tongue, then took it back off. Once it was on the right way, he got a pair of socks out the drawer. These he put on the wrong way as well. Skipping the tongue click, he righted them. A pair of pants were brought out. He held them by the thighs and held them aloft in front of him. He nodded. These were the right way round. And so, after a moment of careful deliberation, he turned them inside out.

Alan smiled, then, realizing what he'd just done, began to frown.

He hadn't noticed it earlier, but his ears were perked, and he kept stealing glances at the door. His heart was thumping like a malfunctioning sledgehammer, and there was a slab of ice in the pit of his stomach. Alan wondered about this, and, his mind as frazzled as it was, it took him two dozen heartbeats to figure out what was going on:

He was scared. Scared that when he opened that door, he'd see that his vision had become reality.

Alan shook his head. This was stupid. That murderer had been playing mind games with him right from the start. Wasn't this what he would be hoping for? That Alan would let his own thoughts destroy him?

But, then again, this guy was the real deal. Alan had seen proof of it. Hell, Gus and Red had seen the fool in action... Well, they *claimed* that they'd seen someone. But since that someone was of Alan's exact description, he was forced to conclude that he had either been set up, or the effects of dementia had whisked away yet another pair of brilliant minds.

Or perhaps he wasn't overthinking at all, just thinking straight.

So, what was Alan to do? The cops? That was far too risky. If the murderer was not bluffing—if he'd *really* planted evidence that pointed to Alan—then it would be over. He, Alan, would get locked up, and there'd be nothing between the murderer and Nala.

"What to do, what to do," Alan said aloud, his head in his hands. And for the next half-cycle of the minute hand around the clock, such he sat, sullen and scared.

When there came a knock on the door, Alan startled so badly that he would have jumped out of his skin had it been a little looser.

"Dad?" Madison said.

"Y-Yes?" he said, his hand on his chest in a futile attempt to calm his racing heart.

"Are you alright, Dad? We heard you drain the tub a while ago. Mom's getting worried out here."

The stupidest smile you could imagine appeared on his face.

She's worried...

That means she's still alive!

The knocks landed louder this time. Following a moment of silence, the door came open and Madison's head poked in. "Dad? What are you up to?"

"Mm? Just... Just thinking, Madison."

"Well, come think out here. It's not good to keep yourself cooped up."

"Yes, yes, I know." And he got off the bed and joined his family in the living room.

"Hey, Asher, Madison?"

"Mm?" They both turned to him in tandem, both unintentionally donning puppy dog eyes, and in that moment they seemed closer to a pair of little toddlers than two adults in college.

A lump formed in Alan's throat. He swallowed several times to do away with it, then said, "Would you two like to sleep in our room for a while?"

"I would!" Madison cried before he had finished.

Asher cast an odd look at his little sister, then said, "Well, I wouldn't."

Madison visibly deflated. "But *why*?" she grumbled.

"Because the two of us aren't babies anymore."

Madison seemed to contemplate this. "Then, what if..." She fell silent, but Alan could still see the clockwork of her mind straining. Suddenly she brightened. "I got..." she said, trailing off. "Nothing."

Alan and Nala snorted with laughter, and Asher groaned and rubbed at his face.

Madison giggled, seeming not at all sorry.

"Anyway, Dad," Asher said. "I'm not gonna sleep with you and Mom, but I'd be fine with sleeping in the next room." He shrugged. "The view from upstairs was getting kinda boring anyway."

"Hm? Oh, yeah, that's fine, Asher," Alan said.

It was a wonderful moment to him, and the only point of the day where he didn't feel close to drowning from stress.

They talked and laughed a little longer, but, little by little, the beauty of the moment began to slip away. By the time the scarlet of the evening sun touched their walls, the knot in his stomach was back, along with all the pressure and paranoia and stealing glances at windows and doors.

And soon enough, night fell.

Alan was shaking

Madison and Asher were making good on their promise. As such, the room beside his and Nala's now had the sound of muffled conversation coming from it. The bed was set right up against the dividing wall, so Alan didn't need to strain his ears to listen.

"Goodnight, kids," Nala was saying, her voice sounding dreamy and far away. "Remember to get a good night's sleep, alright? You're both really young, so you need your rest."

"Yes, Mom, we know." Asher said. "Good night."

"Good night, Mom," Madison said, then a little louder she called, "Goodnight, Dad!"

"Yes, goodnight, Madison. You too, Asher."

Whether Asher responded to that he was unsure. All he could think about was Nala. He had a terrible feeling. He tried to ignore it, but as the day went on it grew and grew. Now, no matter how keen he was on leaving its presence unacknowledged, he had it forced upon him.

Nala would not make it through the night.

Alan shivered as Nala stepped back into the room.

How could it be? Just look how alive she was right now. How could anything possibly happen to steal her away by daybreak?

That wouldn't happen. Not if *he* had anything to say about it.

Alan washed up first, then Nala, and within two minutes they were both lying in bed.

Nala stretched her arms over her head and turned onto her side. She made to stroke the side of his face, only to find that it wasn't where she expected it to be.

"Alan, why are you sitting up?"

"I wanted to write a little. Catch up on my schedule, you know."

"Hmmm." Nala narrowed her eyes at him in suspicion, as though she knew something was being kept from her. She stuck out her bottom lip and shrugged. "Well, if you want to. Just don't stay up too late, alright?"

"Alright. Goodnight, Nala."

"Goodnight, Alan."

Nala fell asleep, but Alan stayed awake. Three quarters of an hour into his idle sitting, he was still wide awake. He had gotten an entire flask of coffee to stave off his sleep, but so far he hadn't needed it. He had so much excess energy, in fact, that for a moment he considered going off on a writing spree. He decided against it, though: What if he missed something important, a noise or a flash?

And so he drew open the curtains and took to gazing upon the flowers of spring, all now petaled and filling the night with their colors. How pretty. At a different phase in his career, he might've dedicated an entire chapter to depicting the way the world beyond the window fell upon his eyes.

He turned to Nala, fast asleep, her hand loosely clenching the edge of her blanket. Alan's heart missed a beat. He wasn't going to let a damn person near her. They could try, and he'd turn them inside out.

Yes, tonight, it was just the two of them.

Still not at all tired, Alan returned his gaze to the window.

And then, as suddenly as if he'd been hit by a truck, he was asleep.

Chapter 20

A dreamless sleep. Alan had never understood how it could happen. The brain, constantly nagging and noticing and getting bored when you were awake, keeping still and silent when there was not a damn other thing for it to be doing? Ridiculous.

And yet, despite any opinions he may have held on the matter, a dreamless sleep was indeed what he had. Although, once or twice, he thought he saw something flash red, like one of those traffic lights that for some reason only possessed one light.

And then there were the noises. Now, what could these have been if not the product of a dream? An odd squelching, and something akin to the cry of a kettle. A kettle. Hm. Had he left something on the stove? No, couldn't be.

But then, still asleep, Alan suddenly remembered something. Perhaps a reflection of his obsession with his career, what fell into his mind was a line in one of his earliest and most well received books. His memory of it was at best paraphrasal, but what he *did* remember was that he'd used the whistle of a kettle to describe another sound: a scream.

A few more flashes of red came and went, only a couple more kettles, and even after everything else was gone, the squelching remained, like the sound of someone stirring around a bucketful of mashed potatoes.

Squelch. Squelch. Squelch.

Silence...

Squelch. Squelch.

And then silence. *Real* silence. Still and unbothered.

Just as suddenly as the truck had run him over, it now backed up, and Alan's consciousness was restored.

His eyes popped open. He was no longer lying in bed but kneeling on the floor. The moonlight fell through the curtain he had drawn and fell on a small part of the floor. Something oddly shaped lay in this patch of pallid light, and for a moment he could not tell what it was.

Something like a ball... And then a spider... And then something that looked as though poor Cupid had had one of his wings snipped off.

Alan squinted, and slowly his eyes adjusted to the darkness. As the seconds drew on, the three objects began to fall on his eyes more and more clearly. At last, he could tell what they were—his heart stopped.

An eye, a hand, and a foot, each surrounded by a small pool of blood and bits and pieces of ground-up muscle.

Nala! What about Nala?!

He looked around hysterically, and in that moment, he looked closer to a mad ape than any human ever had. At last his eyes fell on her. She was in bed, lying on her back, just where he had left her. So peaceful. So beautiful.

Dead.

Right foot, right hand, right eye, all gone. Moonlight illuminated the rag stuffed deep enough into her mouth to have suffocated her and kept any screams she had to offer at bay. It illuminated the terrible gashes and massive lacerations all over her body, blood gushing out of these in such copious amounts that her side of the bed was stained a completely different color to his own.

Alan gasped, but it felt close to empty. Emotionless. As though an amateur actor had been told to gasp, and this was the worst take they managed.

Alan looked around, hoping for his eyes to land on something—*anything*—that showed signs of entry. But there was nothing. The locked door remained locked. The curtains stood proud and unmoved, which would have been impossible had entry been gained through the window, for, if you remember, the windows could not be closed from the outside.

Not the door. Not the window. Those are the only two ways in and out...

Alan froze up, realizing what that must have meant.

Slowly, carefully, he turned around...

Nothing.

A little confused, he threw his gaze about the rest of the room, every nook and cranny, every cupboard, under the bed...

Nobody.

As he had wished, tonight, it had been just the two of them.

Standing in the middle of the moonlit patch, thoroughly confused, his eyes flickered to his scarred hand, perhaps unsure of what else they were supposed to be doing.

His hand was wet. Red. The valleys and the mountains, all red. He looked at his other hand, and it was much of the same.

Alan remained fixated on his hands, shifting his attention from one to the other, like a child who could not decide which slice of cake he wanted more.

His brain churned and grinded like an overheated ceiling fan. Possibilities were crossed out of his mental list, one by one, the impossible and the unlikely. In the end, he was left with just a single option.

All of a sudden, Alan smiled. He had a maniacal urge to laugh, but it stopped at his teeth. After all this time, he finally understood what was going on.

He drew all the curtains, filling the room with moonlight. For a moment he stopped to gaze outside. The sky was gray and cloudless rather than black.

Dawn would come soon.

As he drew the final curtain, he noticed that his blood-dyed hand left a mark. Nala would have never let him hear the end of it. But, luckily, she was away for the moment.

Alan crept over to the dividing wall between his and the kids' room. For a moment he simply stood there, hesitating. Then he pressed his ear to it. His gag work had been exceptional, it seemed: he could hear Asher and Madison's soft breathing. Light sleepers though they were, they had managed to sleep through a murder happening not one room off.

Alan peeled away from the wall and got his satchel from the nightstand. From inside he pulled out his pencils and his book; it was no longer smooth and thin, but rather a little bloated, the way all books that saw their purpose inevitably wound up.

He brought these over to his study, drew the chair with a terrible scrape—who cared if he drew attention now?—and got to work. There was hardly a tenth of the pages left blank; this would be the final chapter.

As he leafed through the remaining pages, counting them aloud, he noticed a rip in one of them. A small but deliberate rip. He eyed it a moment, and something in his head seemed to click. He rummaged through his satchel. It was small, so perhaps he had lost it. But still he rummaged, and rummaged, and rummaged...

And a good thing he did, for not a minute later his fingers found it.

It was the little piece of paper he'd found in that envelope all that time ago. The one that bore the number to that murderer's phone.

Alan held the little piece of paper up to the rip—and he chuckled. Sure enough, a perfect match.

Alan threw aside the paper and picked up his pencil.

As he wrote, his hand jotting down the words before his brain had finished generating them, he kept chuckling to himself.

Alan Michaels, how could you have been so stupid?

A car passed by. *A rather suspicious hour*, Alan thought. Probably one of the neighbors.

He wondered. Wondered if they knew that, all this time, there had been a killer on the block? Could they have known that, in the time that they'd been having their beauty sleep, their neighborhood had gone one inhabitant shorter?

No, of course they couldn't have known!

Alan shivered in excitement. He was the first to know! Not the neighbors, not her children, nor her parents... Hell, probably not even God Himself knew. But him? Oh, he, Alan Michaels, was different. He knew. And that feeling, the feeling of being alone on the mountain, nearly made him burst with pleasure.

"But," he said aloud, "it would've been a hell of a lot better under a streetlight."

His left hand kept writing, but his eyes were no longer on the sheet before him, but on a certain point out the window, something he thought he could see. But, of course he couldn't see it: the place was a couple of miles away, for crying out loud.

A streetlight, ay? came a very familiar voice in his head. *Why? Feeling a pull to the good old days, Michaels?*

Alan smiled. "You bet, Michaels." He chuckled. "Quite the bit of cardio, huh? How many trips was that, to and fro. A dozen?"

More, I'd guess.

"What, like, fifteen, maybe?" Alan shrugged. "All that to go sit in some decrepit station, go talk on some payphone that doesn't even work."

I was wondering when you'd figure it out. That accident tore the insanity out of you. The drunken mess. What a damn shame. You have no idea how long I was waiting for you to find me.

"Well, you can't blame me for that. Up until just now, I'd completely forgotten that I'd ever been a drunk."

You're a fool, Michaels. Why do you think the youngest began looking around the table at the diner a while back, going as pale as snow? Because she was looking for the booze, looking for the gas that used to fuel your beating them. You used to beat them, all three of them. You know that much, at least?

"I'm aware. Also," Alan said rather sharply. "For no logical reason, first damn thing you do, right after leaving that diner that first time? You kill that florist, chuck her in that old station, then cut the wires on all the payphones. I remember it now."

I was trying to remind you of who you are. You ain't no damn goody two shoes, and I was trying to show you that. I even took the trouble to draw flowers on her face to try and remind you. Hell, I even left a number in an envelope at your favorite table at the diner to call to try and spark your memory of me. Do you remember it now? That other killer's trademark, the one that Gus and Red were talking about when you first got this nutty idea?

Alan nodded matter-of-factly. "Symmetry."

Damn right, symmetry. Do you realize why I killed her, specifically, and not some other wench?

Alan shrugged. "Beats me."

Her name's Nala. Different culture and different intonation, but Nala nonetheless. You remember how thoroughly we used to perform our beatings? You're a fool if you think any of my punches were not thought out.

"You're a fool for thinking that I knew you were me."

It was obvious.

"No, it sure as hell w—" Alan cut himself off to curse. The blood on his hands was dry, and a large chunk of it flaked off and landed on the page. Alan wiped it away, leaving a dry red rainbow on the page.

"Anyway, an odd symmetry, the third and fourth kills, no? Butcher the left of one, the right of the other. Well, I guess if you tape 'em together, it *is* symmetry, in a way. The mannequin parts at that pink-haired guy's house, was that some sort of foreshadowing?"

Yes, it was. Thank you for noticing. How much you got left?

Alan turned to gaze out the window. The sky was whitening, shifting from dark gray to a very, very pale gray.

"I'll be done by the time the sun begins to peek," Alan said.

That's good. Why aren't you washing your hands? You'll write a lot quicker without all the blood mucking things up.

"Nah, it's fine. It'll take too long, and I'll lose my flow." Alan placed his pencil down for a moment, stretched, then got back to it.

The pages flew past. Soon there were only four pages left, front and back.

A car rumbled past, reminding Alan of the time. He shot a glance at the window; the faintest whisper of violet lay all across the horizon.

So, once you're done with this, what are you gonna do? You gonna publish?

"I'm not too sure, honestly. My initial thought was to publish, but now this feels a little too personal for me to be willing. A little too... Well, incriminating. I'll feel pretty stupid if I get locked up over some cop or somebody reading this."

I hear ya, Michaels.

Alan looked outside. The sky looked as though it was burning with all its violent scarlet and orange, and yet the sun was not yet up.

A little more, just a little more...

Three things happened at the exact same moment:

The crow of a rooster rent the silent air of dawn;

The sun at last came peeking over the horizon;

And Alan Michael's freshly-blunted pencil gave a satisfying click as it was set onto the study.

His book was complete.

Done, Michaels?

Alan did not respond to the voice. Instead, he shut the book and held it up, looking in that moment like a parent holding up their newborn. He pushed away from the table and went over to Nala's bloody, mangled corpse.

He smiled, touched the book to her forehead, then leaned in and kissed her on the cheek.

"Thank you for everything, Nala." He shut her one remaining eye with the palm of his hand. "That's enough for one lifetime."

He planted one final kiss on her left hand, just the way he did the day he swore, "'Til death do us part."

"Goodnight."